"Here! what's this rolling across the floor?"

(Page 142)

THE STORY OF
THE MINCE PIE

BY
JOSEPHINE SCRIBNER GATES
Author of "Captain Billie," "The Story of Live Dolls,"
"Little Girl Blue," etc.

ILLUSTRATED BY
JOHN RAE

NEW YORK
DODD, MEAD AND COMPANY
1916

THE MINCE PIE has always held an important place in Christmas Tales, but it remained for Mrs. Mildred G. Potter to conceive the idea of making it the main feature.

It is my pleasure to give to her my grateful acknowledgment for the happy thought which it has been my privilege to embody in story form.

> Here's to the Dolls that will come to life,
> Here's to the Tales they'll tell
> Out of the depths of the Christmas Pie,
> To the tune of a Christmas Bell!
>
> Here's to the Sugar and Fruit and Spice,
> Here's to the Story Elf,
> Here's to that Fragrance of Christmas Time,
> Here's to the Pie itself!
>
> Big and spicy and rich and brown,
> What does that top crust hide?
> You know how it looks from an outside view,
> Now read what it's like inside!

BY
DOT AND NICK
WHO ALSO WANTED A FINGER
IN THIS PIE!

J. S. G.

CONTENTS

	PAGE
THE MINCE PIE	1
RAISIN DOLL	10
CURRANT DOLL	18
CLOVE DOLL	21
DANCE OF THE ELVES	26
SPRITE'S TALE	27
ALLSPICE DOLL	37
NUTMEG DOLL	39
CINNAMON DOLL	42
PIED PIPER STORY	46
MRS. SUGAR	60
MOLASSES DOLL	66
VINEGAR KING	70
CITRON DOLL	74
TALES OF THE ORANGE AND LEMON DOLLS	76
ANNA BELLE'S CHRISTMAS EVE	79
TALES OF THE SALT AND PEPPER TWINS	104
APPLE DOLL	108
JOHNNY APPLESEED	110
STOLEN DOLL CLOTHES	129
BROWNIE DOLL	134
PIE CRUST	142
HOW JACK FILLED THE STOCKINGS	146
INTERROGATION POINT	157

ILLUSTRATIONS

"Here! what's this rolling across the floor?" *Frontispiece* (Page 142)

	FACING PAGE
"They've been peeking in that big book"	8
"Behold, the Story Sprite!"	16
"Great sport they had flying wonderful kites"	28
"We will both wish for her to come"	36
"The beauty of the scene almost overwhelmed him"	50
"Sometimes it is gingerbread, or maybe plump brown cookies"	60
"Suddenly something startled the horse, and he ran away"	70
"She was making dolls from bottles"	82
"'Show what we are to take,' cried the Fairy. 'We must hurry'"	94
"I am used very extensively as an April Fool"	104
"The children sat at his feet and listened to thrilling tales"	112
"They looked like a lot of gnomes dressed for a party"	122
"She loved her home"	134
"He chose the busiest corner where there was a wonderful toy store"	148
"Best pie you ever made, my dear"	160

"Sing a Song o' sixpence a pocket full of rye,
Four and twenty Dollies baked in a pie,
When the pie was opened the Dolls began to sing,
Wasn't that an odd dish to set before the King?"

You have heard of many kinds of pie, but did you ever hear of a Doll pie?

No one ever did, I am sure, and no one knew the pie was full of dolls; everybody supposed it was just a plain mince pie; the kind that makes your eyes twinkle, and makes you smack your lips when you sniff it baking.

I have always thought it was the kind Jack Horner had when he sat in the corner and pulled out a plum, but never did I dream that he might have pulled out a doll!

THE STORY OF

I found it out in such an extremely funny and unexpected way that I must tell you all about it.

It was Christmas Eve. Jack's father was away but coming home on the morrow in time for all the Christmas doings.

We had locked up the house and were just going upstairs to bed when Jack exclaimed:

"Mother, you know the mince pie you baked to-day? We must take it up to bed with us!"

"A pie, a mince pie to bed with us?" I cried in amazement, as I thought of the spicy delicious thing safely stowed away on the pantry shelf.

"Yes, Mother, you know there is a mouse. It ate up my gingerbread doll; didn't leave even a crumb. How would we feel if it ate up our mince pie!"

That was true. There had been a mouse

THE MINCE PIE

spying about of late, and so I said all right, we would.

I carried it up very carefully, and we stood in the middle of the room looking about for a good place to put it.

It was a bitter night. The maid had built a grand fire of logs, and they crackled and snapped a Christmas greeting as we stood seeking a resting place for the pie.

"I see a fine spot!" cried Jack, as he ran to the big grandfather clock, and sure enough it was. A shelf just under the pendulum that seemed made on purpose for a pie. We placed it there and covered it carefully with a napkin.

"The pie is going to bed, too," I said, as I snuggled it up under its cover.

Jack shouted over this, and we both had a merry time undressing before the jolly fire.

We hung up our stockings and one for Father, then hopped into bed.

THE STORY OF

Jack nestled up close and begged for a bedtime story, which I always told him. A drowsy tale which sent him to sleep, and me, too, before it was barely finished.

I really didn't know I was asleep, but suddenly a queer sound startled me, and as I listened I heard Jack smothering a giggle.

"What is it, dear?" I whispered.

"Oh, Mother, such a funny thing! I heard the clock chain rattle, and I looked and the mouse ran up the clock, and I heard voices singing: 'Hickory Dickory Dock.' Now look quick!"

We both stared at the napkin over the pie, for it began to get humpy. You have played "tent" under the bedclothes, of course.

Well, there seemed a dozen somethings playing that game, for the napkin humped up here and there till presently it was lifted off and fell to the floor.

THE MINCE PIE

It was just like a matinée. The napkin seemed to be the curtain rolled away, then the show began.

We heard queer voices singing, and then we saw such a sight! Out of that pie filed a lot of dolls, the strangest looking dolls any one ever saw.

One seemed to be made of raisins; another of currants—the dried sugary kind. One had a round apple for a head, and such rosy cheeks it looked like a blooming country maid wearing a Dutch blue gown and an apron as white as snow.

Back of her was a brownie, holding the hand of a creamy white fat boy. Following them was a group, one had a round nut-like head; another was stuck full of what looked like cloves; another was tall and thin just like a stick. With him was a pair of twins. They looked for all the world like salt and pepper boxes. They were much

THE STORY OF

smaller than the others and teetered on the edge of the pie like tiny fairies.

Then came another pair, one with an orange for a head, the other a lemon. As they pranced along, their fluffy orange and yellow skirts stood out like ballet dancers.

Then came a dumpy maid all sparkly white.

"She's the shape of a fat sugar bowl, Mother!" whispered Jack, and, sure enough, she looked as though she had walked right off the tea tray.

Following her came one with a small oval brown head, looking so wise.

With her was one with a large green head.

Back of them strode another pair; one looking like a molasses jug, the other like a vinegar cruet.

Such a funny lot as they were!

We looked and laughed, and laughed and looked. They raced about on the very edge

THE MINCE PIE

of the crust as though they were playing Ring around a Rosy; then at a signal from the tall thin fellow they ran down the spiral column of the clock over to the hearth.

"We can have a Christmas dance right here," cried the rosy-cheeked apple maid; at this joyful news they switched off their sashes.

The tall thin one fastened the ends to the top of an andiron, and there in the firelight we saw a dance, such as no one ever saw before. Round and round they danced, till the iron was bound with ribbon to its very base; then the little creatures threw themselves on the hearth.

"Let's play school!" cried the tall thin Stick Doll, who seemed to be chairman for the occasion.

"Mercy, no!" cried another. "I don't like school. I don't want to learn things."

'I said let's *play* school. We don't have

THE STORY OF

to learn anything. It will be fun. We'll each tell a story."

"A story!" echoed the whole bunch.

"What kind of a story?"

"A true story."

"We don't know any," they all sighed.

"Oh, yes, you do. You all know fine stories, and if you'll tell them, something grand is going to happen!"

"What?" cried the audience.

"This is the one night of all the year when wonderful things happen."

With wide open eyes and mouths they crept closer to the speaker, and listened breathlessly.

"This is Christmas Eve. Didn't you hear the mouse go up the clock? It's hiding and watching. Pretend you aren't looking, but see the two bright eyes peering at us, just at the end by the big hand. It wants the pie.

"They've been peeking in that big book"

THE MINCE PIE

As long as we are here it will not come down. That is a Christmas pie for the Christmas dinner to-morrow.

"If we go back the mouse will run down and gobble us all up. So there is nothing for us to do but stay here. It's a long time till morning, and we better do something while we wait. How can we better while away the time than with stories? We dare not go to sleep, you know. If you'll each tell a story you can have a gift, too."

"A gift!" cried the chorus. "Well, that would be worth while. Pray tell us what will the gift be?"

"That's a secret I am not allowed to tell. The reason is, because I do not know."

"He does not know. He does not know," sang the chorus, running down the scale as a mouse runs across the piano keys.

"Well," cried the wee Salt and Pepper

TALE OF THE

Pair which seemed inseparable, "since you know so much, you better begin the story-hour."

"I speak to be the teacher," cried the Raisin Doll.

"Very well, you must tell the first story, then."

"What must the stories be about?"

"Oh, there is only one thing to tell. We must each tell our history from the time we were born, in order to have the gift."

"Will the gift be good to eat?" asked the creamy white Fat Boy.

"Best ever you tasted. That's all I could find out about it. Now begin."

The Raisin Doll pranced over to the end of the hearth, made a quick bow, and politely began:

"Ladies and Gentlemen:"

Everybody giggled, but he went bravely on.

RAISIN DOLL

"I don't seem to remember the day I was born."

"Not many do," whispered one to another.

"It isn't polite to interrupt," frowned the speaker.

"The first thing I remember a whole bunch of us was hanging from a vine—"

"Ha! Ha! Ha!" shouted the chorus. "A whole bunch of him was hanging from a vine!"

"Well, there was a whole bunch of us, and as I looked about I saw many bunches and many, many vines.

"It was beautiful there in the sunlight. I never saw such glorious sunshine—"

"Where?" cried the audience.

"In a place called California."

"Where is that?" asked one.

"Don't tell us; we don't want to know," hastily cried the audience. "We aren't to learn things here in this school."

TALE OF THE

"I won't tell you. I'll show you," and the speaker hopped on to the large globe that stood in the corner.

He slid down one side and placed his big toe on the spot where California claimed to be.

They all watched his antics closely, for in their hearts they did want to know where those bunches of grapes grew, even though they didn't seem to want to learn anything.

"That's exactly where my bunch of grapes grew, but I have cousins called Malagas and Muscatels who come from Spain.

"You don't want to know where that is, of course. I am now going to take a little run around the world. Pretend I'm a top spinning, and the spot where I stop and twirl will be where my relatives live. When it's time to twirl I'll squeak and you can then close your eyes for the moment, so you won't add anything to your store of knowledge.

RAISIN DOLL

"For my part, I would feel quite pleased if I were sailing around the world and could say, 'Oh, Mr. Captain, just stop a few moments in Mediterranean Spain. I want a pocket full of raisins to eat; the layer kind, big fat juicy ones'; or if I were pudding hungry I'd wheedle him a little. I'd say, 'Now, Captain dear, I'd just like to run into Valencia. We need a few pudding raisins. We'll have a pudding that'll melt in your mouth if we can go there.'

"I think that's much better than to stand around with my mouth open, and when we steam into these places be wondering what grows there, and why we stopped."

That was a new idea. Journeys on ships were fun, and how proud one would feel to be able to show the Captain just where to go for certain things.

"Mother," whispered Jack, "let's watch where he twirls. Maybe a captain might even beg us to go and show him where raisins grow, so he can bring back a shipload of them!"

The Raisin Doll now skipped gaily along as though he were going to the corner grocery for a stick of candy.

The audience gazed fascinated, and instead of closing eyes as he squeaked, they hardly dared wink for fear they might miss some of that raisin country.

"Where is he now?" one and another whispered as he paused and twirled, crying:

"There! There is the very spot where many of my cousins live, and because they live there instead of in California they are much sweeter."

"Tell us why, tell us why," clamoured the audience.

"For a very good reason. We are picked in bunches and dried in an oven in sugar. They are dried in the sun, and are called

RAISIN DOLL

sun raisins. Their leaves are taken off, and a jolly time they have in the sunshine and fresh air. A much better way than to be shut in an oven in the dark.

"However, we have to make the best of it; the cool nights and heavy dews would ruin us if we stayed out, so we just cuddle up in the nice warm dark, and look forward to the moment when the big oven door will fly open, then we know something nice is to happen, for America sends millions of pounds of raisins to other countries, and we just love to go.

"The sun raisins are the kind used for Christmas goodies, and are packed between layers of paper in large wooden boxes.

"Other places they come from are here, and here, and here, and here."

As he spoke, he twirled over various parts of the globe, touching Persia, Greece, Italy, and Southern France.

"It is quite grand to be a sun raisin and

TALE OF THE

come in a box looking so large and delicious, and to know you are the finest of your kind, but I'd just about as soon be a pudding raisin, when the Cook comes in and says:

" 'Dear suz me, Missus, we can't have pudding to-day!'

"Then all the children set up a dismal wail and Missus says, 'Why not, I'd like to know!'

" 'Because we are just out of pudding raisins,' but she adds cheerfully, 'We have the layer kind. Could we use those?'

" 'Certainly not,' says the Missus, with her head up like this and her mouth turned down like this. 'They cost too much. We'll have to have something else.'

"Then at dinner the Mister cries, 'Why didn't we have pudding to-day; we always have it on Tuesday!'

" 'Cause no pudding raisins in the house,' cry the children, sniffing again.

"Behold, the Story Sprite!"

RAISIN DOLL

"'Send for a barrel of them,' orders the Mister. 'When that gives out, get another at once. When I have my mouth made up for pudding on Tuesdays I don't want to be disappointed.'

"Wouldn't that make a cute little pudding raisin hug herself?

"Another kind of raisin grows here in Smyrna; they are the small seedless kind."

"The Corinthian raisin currant—"

"Boo! hoo! hoo!" interrupted somebody, apparently much grieved.

"Who's crying like that?" asked the Raisin Doll.

"I am," came in sobbing tones.

"Why?" asked everybody, standing on tip toe to see the weeping one.

"He's telling my story. There isn't much to tell about me, and if he tells it, I can't; then I won't get a gift!"

"To be sure you won't!" said the tall Stick

TALE OF THE

Doll. "Mr. Raisin, are you going to tell everybody's story, may I ask?"

"Why, no," said the Raisin Doll, a bit fussed over the uproar; "I forgot that one of my cousins was present.

"Allow me to introduce to you the light-hearted, joyous-natured Corinthian raisin Currant."

The light-hearted, joyous-natured Currant Doll wiped his tears away as he bowed and wailed:

"Ladies and Gentlemen, I am, though maybe I don't look it."

"Am what?" queried the audience sympathetically.

"Am what he said—light hearted and gay —and though my story is short I am just as important as any of you. What good would a bun be without currants? Just tell me that!" he cried in tragic tones, striking such

CURRANT DOLL

a funny attitude even Mother stifled a giggle.

"I came from a beautiful vine that grows in the lowlands of Zante of the Ionian Islands belonging to Greece. I'll show you the very spot."

Here the audience was much surprised to see the light-hearted creature turn a somersault down the slippery side of the globe and land in a nest of small dots.

"These are islands," he announced, "and here the vines are planted in neat little rows three feet apart. Our grapes are like berries no larger than a pea, and grow in clusters about three inches long.

"When about three years old the vine produces bunches of three kinds; red, black, and white grapes without seeds. We play hide and seek under the large leaves which protect us from the strong winds and hot sun.

"When we have grown as large as we can we are picked, dried, packed, and sent many miles away. That's all."

And he sat down so hard he bounced up again like a rubber ball.

"Three cheers for the Currant!" cried the Stick Doll. "He seems to have grown up under the figure three, and that brings good luck.

"Now, who wants to tell next?"

Nobody moved, and the Stick Doll cried:

"We'll decide it by playing Ring around a Rosy. The last one down will be it. Come, hold hands, circle, and sing."

Round and round they went, singing to an accompaniment of rollicking laughter, and at the words: "Hush, hush, hush, we all fall down," they fell in a heap, the Clove Doll being the last to fall.

"Allow me," cried the Stick Doll, as he gallantly set Miss Clove on her feet.

CLOVE DOLL

"We will now have the pleasure of listening to this spicy creature. She surely has a fine story to tell."

Miss Clove had been slyly studying the dictionary, and longed to impress the audience with the wonderful story of her life. She smoothed her crimson sash, perked the butterfly bow on her hair till it seemed almost ready to fly away, and with cheeks as red as her ribbons began timidly.

"Ladies and Gentlemen: I am an undeveloped bud—"

"Ha! Ha!" cried one, who looked much like a vinegar cruet. "That is a joke!"

"Why?" demanded the Stick Doll.

"She said undeveloped."

"So she did, what of it? You may tell us what the word means."

The sour-looking one, much confused, stalked away as he murmured under his breath,

"We aren't to learn anything here, I thought."

"No, but if you knew the meaning of it, you would answer very promptly, so the joke is on you. The speaker can, of course, tell us."

The Clove Doll's cheeks flushed even redder than before, and wished with all her heart she had not used the large word of which she was so proud.

"I am sure I cannot tell what it means. It's what I am, and it's the way my story begins."

"Who knows what the very large word used by the very small one means?" asked the Stick Doll, of the audience.

The Pepper and Salt Twins now stepped forward. They swayed from side to side and in sing-song tones cried:

"Un means not. Undeveloped means not developed; developed means finished."

CLOVE DOLL

"Excellent memory you have," said the Stick Doll.

"They've been peeking in that big book, too; I saw them," cried the Vinegar Cruet. "Any one could do that."

"Tell tale tit, your tongue shall be slit," sang the whole crowd.

"Here! Here! This won't do. Come, let us hear the rest of the story of this unfinished maid."

"It isn't true that I am not finished! As a clove I am complete and perfect. It is only that the buds are used before they are quite ready to turn into blossoms.

"If my buds were allowed to blossom there would never be a clove. What would the pickled peach do then, poor thing?"

"She'd stay in her jar,
And soon be sour,
And moulder away on the shelf, poor thing!"

promptly sang the audience.

At this Jack and Mother hid their heads in the blankets, shaking with laughter, and came forth with very red faces just in time to hear Miss Clove continue her spicy tale.

"The clove tree grows in the woods in hot countries, specially here and here, and here."

"She's on roller skates," whispered Jack, as the Clove Lady sailed quickly and gracefully around the globe, touching with her wheeled feet Zanzibar, Brazil, and the West Indies.

"The audience need not note especially the countries pointed out," said the Stick Doll, "but it is to me most interesting. You may continue."

The Clove Doll had snatched the moment while she waited to again improve her mind through the big book, and now announced importantly:

"I am very pungent. That means aromatic."

CLOVE DOLL

"Oh!" cried the Vinegar Cruet, "you had to shut the book too quick to find the meaning of that, but I happen to know it.

"Why are you like me?"

"Happy thought," said the Stick Doll; "let's turn this into a puzzle contest. Why is the clove like vinegar?"

"Give it up. Give it up. What's the answer?" sang the audience.

"Because we are both sharp," politely answered the Vinegar Cruet, strutting about like a peacock.

"Sharp! Ha! Ha!" cried Pepper and Salt. "S'pose you've been visiting the scissors' grinder."

"Vinegar is right," said the Clove Doll. "We are both smart."

"Ha! Ha! Ha! Ha! Let's all carry a pocket dictionary and we can be smart and sharp, too," laughed some one.

"Dear me!" cried the Clove Doll. "Did I

DANCE OF THE ELVES

really say smart? I mis-spoke. I am sharp. I mean stinging to the tongue."

Before she could say another word she was surrounded and tested so vigorously by the many tongues, she shrieked indignantly:

"Stop! we don't lick the ladder till the ice cream is done. Now let me finish.

"My buds turn green, then red and hard. Then we are laid near the smoke of a wood fire in the sun to dry. We don't like that smudge and are glad enough when we turn brown, then we know we are finished. I might say developed," she added, with a triumphant glance at her hearers.

"The last night there in the woods we had a grand time. We looked like a lot of elves dancing in the red glow shed by the fire.

"I'll never forget what happened that night. We had just finished a weird dance and were huddled together watching the sparks mount to the sky, when there ap-

SPRITE'S TALE

peared in our midst a queer little Being, who seemed to spring from the fire.

"She seated herself in our midst and told us the grandest stories I ever heard!"

"Oh!" cried Allspice, "I wish she would come here!"

At that instant they heard a far-off voice. It seemed to come from the flames. Singing, singing, nearer and nearer.

Suddenly from the very centre of the fire sprang a wonderful vision, a tiny creature, who seemed clothed in wreaths of flame. With a joyous greeting, as jolly as the fire itself, she cried:

"Your wish is granted. Behold, the Story Sprite! Since I attended the clove party I have been around the world and have a fine collection of tales.

"I am fresh from Japan, now, where I saw enacted a most exciting tale. Creep close to my feet while I tell it. I wish you could

THE STORY

see the children in Japan. They are so beautiful; clad in their brilliant coloured kimonos, they look like a mass of poppies nodding in the wind.

"One dear little Japanese maid did such a splendid thing!

"Without speaking a word, with only her dear two hands, she saved a young man from being imprisoned for life. He was an American gentleman, who had been sent to Japan on business.

"He was lonely so far from home, and became very friendly with Cherry Blossom, the child of one with whom he had business relations.

"He was very much interested in the queer games she played, and spent much time with her.

"Great sport they had flying wonderful kites that looked like gorgeous birds with outspread wings, or maybe seated on the

"Great sport they had flying wonderful kites"

SPRITE'S TALE

beach she would make sand pictures, which were her great delight.

"They usually wound up these visits with a tea-party. The child seated opposite him, looking like a brilliant butterfly, poised for a moment as she handed him the fragile cup filled with the fragrant beverage.

"In time he became very dear to her, and one day while playing with her dolly she overheard something that sorely troubled her little heart. Her father was talking in low mysterious tones to some Japanese friends. Suddenly she heard the American's name. She pricked up her ears.

"Dear! Dear! Such startling news she could hardly believe.

"They thought he was a spy and were going to put him in prison very soon! They walked away, leaving the child grief-stricken.

"What a spy was, she did not know; but

THE STORY

what she did know was that her precious friend must be saved from that awful fate, for once in prison he might never be released.

"He had told her of his own little girl, who was even now, in that far away land called America, watching for his home coming. As she gazed off seaward she saw a ship that might sail any day. He must go on it and she must tell him why, but how could she?

"Never was she allowed to be alone with him for one moment. Always when playing her childish games with him, her nurse sat near by, within hearing of her voice, her beady eyes watching her every movement.

"As the child pondered on this startling state of affairs, her friend suddenly appeared. At once the nurse glided to her post.

" 'See the ship,' he cried in her native lan-

SPRITE'S TALE

guage. 'It will sail this evening. The next ship that comes will take me home to my baby. Let's go and buy her a doll.'

"To the shop they went, the nurse trotting along beside them.

"They bought a wonderful doll, an exact copy of Cherry Blossom in her silken robes.

"They bought many other toys, among them a complete outfit for making sand pictures.

" 'I'll tell my baby how you helped me to choose her doll. Now let's go to the beach and you bring your sand bags and teach me how to make the pictures so I can make them for her.'

"Happy thought! Now maybe she could have an instant, just a weenty instant alone with him, and so she asked the nurse to bring the bags of sand.

" 'You come, too,' whispered the nurse, and refused to budge without the child.

THE STORY

"Japanese children must be obedient, and she followed, not even daring to allow her little feet to lag or to seem disturbed in any way.

"She was soon seated on the beach close beside her friend, while the nurse sat a little apart knitting, her eyes fixed on the pair.

"Making pictures in the sand is a wonderful game, a game the Japanese children adore.

"They have three bags of coloured sand and one of white. It is most fascinating to see them spread in the form of a square the white sand, till it resembles a sheet of white paper. On this with black and red, yellow or blue, they produce wonderful landscape effects.

"Cherry Blossom plunged her hands into the bags, her thoughts far away from the game.

"Suddenly her eyes flashed. She knew

how to give him the message. Why hadn't she thought of it before! Pictures could tell most anything, and so she eagerly began.

"Immediately from her tiny fingers the varicoloured sand trickled in a thin stream.

"At first as he idly watched, he saw in her picture a bit of sea, on which presently appeared a ship with spreading sail. On the fluffy white waves, creeping up to the shore, rocked a tiny boat. On the land appeared a prison, a perfect copy of one he had seen many times. In the small boat an American was seated.

"The man watched in tense silence. The child was telling him something. He lit a cigarette with unsteady hands, but as he remembered the sentinel on guard, he began to hum a tune.

"The child's hands never trembled as she next produced a number of Japanese gentlemen.

THE STORY

"Now the man disappeared from the boat, and at once was seen peering through the prison bars.

"Just here the nurse suspiciously drew near to see the picture.

"The man quickly pointed to the sky, crying gaily, 'See the birds!'

"As the nurse gazed skyward, one swift stroke of his hand destroyed the picture, and he said quietly:

" 'Now let me make one. You do them so well I am afraid you will think I am a bungler, but I want to try.'

"As he worked, he whistled a merry tune, and the child felt that he meant her to know he understood. She soon saw that he, too, was picturing a message, for in the twinkling of an eye he had fashioned a tree, its green branches stretching out over the white background.

"On a low branch he placed a bird. It

SPRITE'S TALE

seemed to be making an effort to free itself from a thong which held its little foot. From its beak fluttered a banner. Under his fingers this banner was soon transfigured into an American flag.

"As the man worked, the merry tune was replaced by sharp twitters and chirps as though the bird were distressed.

"The child watched fascinated, as underneath the tree she saw a Japanese child taking shape. Her fingers rested on the bird's foot, and suddenly by a quick twirl of his hand the bird was blotted out and in an instant plainly to be seen poised on the mast of a ship, carolling a glad song of freedom.

"Then the picture was swept away, and with one look into the child's beautiful eyes, a look that told volumes, he gathered up his purchases and sauntered away.

"In his room he hastily packed his belong-

TALE OF THE

ings, and later on under cover of the darkness he was safely stowed on the ship.

"As Cherry Blossom drowsily closed her eyes she heard the ship's shrill whistle as it steamed away, and she rejoiced that she had been able with her own little hands to send her dear friend back to his baby.

"There was great excitement the next day when it was learned the American had vanished.

"The nurse was closely questioned. Never had she left the child alone, and her mother also declared that she too had been on guard, and all she saw was that they made pictures in the sand without even a word.

"And so the secret never was told till now, and it will still be a secret, for pie people never never tell, and now good-bye till you wish for me again."

With a graceful courtesy the Story Sprite vanished as suddenly as she had appeared,

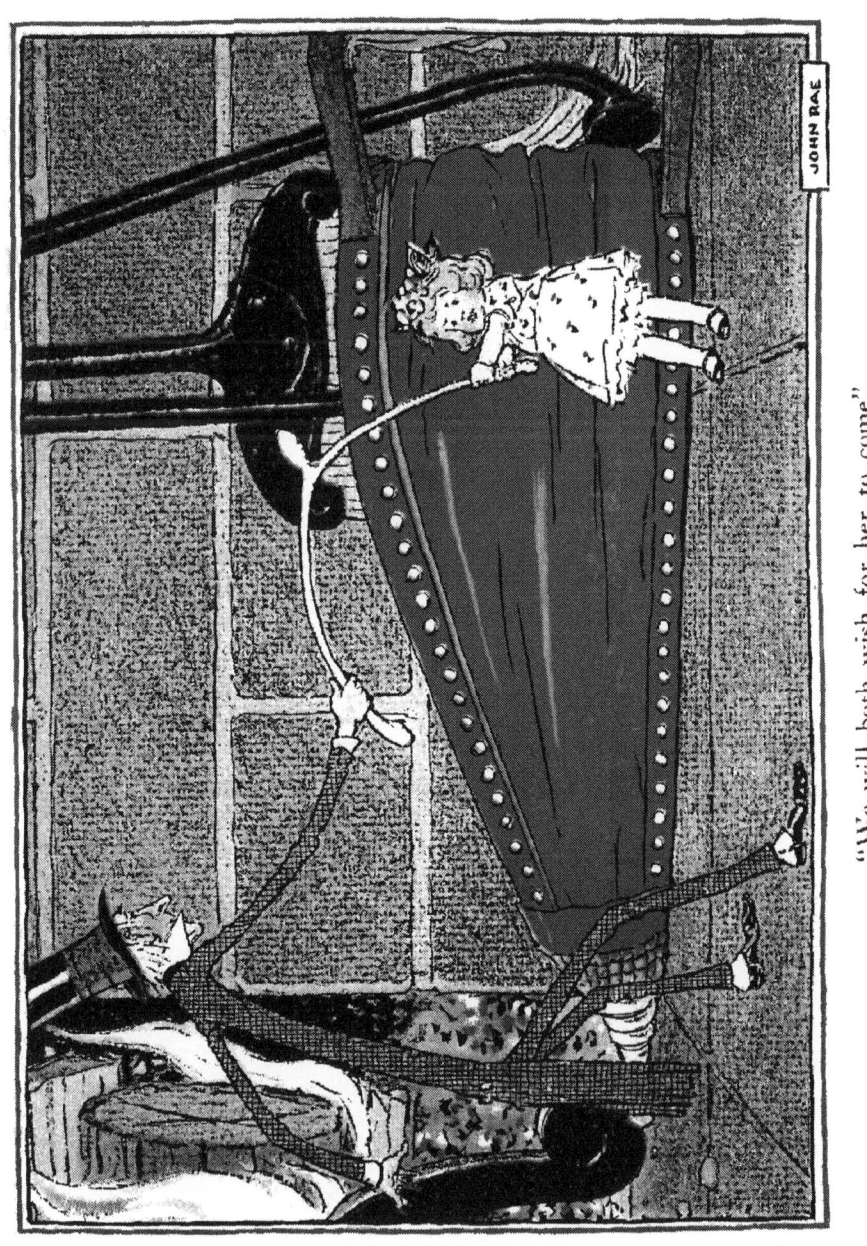

"We will both wish for her to come"

ALLSPICE DOLL

and the audience sat for a moment listening spellbound to her song fast dying away.

Then long-drawn breaths were heard and the Clove Doll cried, "Wasn't she perfect? I never dreamed she would come here, but I am glad she did.

"Now will my cousin, Miss Allspice, please step forward and tell her story."

This dear little doll timidly made her way back of the speaker, and, holding shyly to her skirt, peeped out, and said in low tones:

"I am just a small round berry from the Pimento. A wee evergreen tree that grows on the limestone hills, on the Islands of the West Indies.

"We are about the size of a pea, gathered in August, and dried in the sun for several days. The stems are then taken off and we are packed in a bag and sent to America.

"There such a thing happened to us as you

would never believe possible. We were turned out of the bags, looking like a lot of dried hard peas. We were so happy to be at the end of our journey, and see daylight again.

"We smiled up at the blue sky as we merrily rolled out of the sacks, but, alas, our joy was only for a moment, as we found ourselves turned into a grinder of some sort. Suddenly we heard a whizzing sound, and there we had turned from peas into a fine powder.

"They named us Allspice because we have the flavour of cinnamon, nutmeg, and cloves, and everybody loves us."

Out of breath, the modest little creature completely vanished in Clove's skirt, blown there by the applause which now filled the room.

"Well done!" cried the Stick Doll. "You mean a lot if you are small. Now I think

NUTMEG DOLL

we should hear from the Nutmeg, since spice seems to hold our attention at present."

The doll with the small brown head now arose and walked over to the place of honour. She was a study in green. Her gown was formed of leaves from the tree upon which she grew, and an artistic picture she made as she faced her audience.

"My dear friends," she said, and paused.

"I take my pen in hand to say I am well—" came in an audible whisper.

"And hope you are the same," flashed the Nutmeg. "I admit I was a bit flurried. But thanks to your hurried letter just received I am myself again. I need to be, for I am rather interesting.

"I come chiefly from the Banda Islands, and some of my poor relations come from the West Indies and Brazil, where dear little Allspice lives.

"She forgot to welcome you to her home

and I will show you where it is," and she took from her pocket some tiny round balls and tossed them in various directions.

To the surprise of all, the balls lodged and stuck, and the onlookers were so interested in learning whether they stuck where they should they forgot they weren't to learn anything.

"They did!" whispered Jack and Mother in one breath, and, sure enough, some lodged in the Banda Islands, others in the West Indies.

"Some of us live in South America," and she lightly tossed a few more balls, all of which clung to their native lands.

"What do you mean by poor relations?" asked the Stick Doll.

"I mean the poorer quality of nutmegs. The Brazilian nutmeg brings oil for hard soap and candles.

"I am the better quality, and am the ker-

NUTMEG DOLL

nel of a fruit which is round and about the size of a walnut.

"The outside coat is two inches across before it splits open, and the nutmeg, of course, comes out, just as the chestnut falls from the burr. A network of tiny fibres is wound about it, and this second coat is dried and ground and called mace.

"The olive-shaped nut, about an inch in length, is turned over every day for two months, and treated with lime to preserve it. Then it is the nutmeg which you see before you."

"What are you good for, please, Mam?" asked the Vinegar Cruet with a sour expression.

"What am I good for?" she cried indignantly. "What am I not good for? Look in the cook-book on the pantry shelf and see if there is anything worth while that hasn't a dash of me in it.

"You'll find every good housewife has one of me in a tiny grater hanging where she can find it in the dark. Your puddings, and pies, and gingerbreads, and cakes, and blancmanges, and egg noggs, and—"

"Here! Here! my dear lady, we can't wait to let you go through the whole cook-book. We'll take your word for it. Now since I seem to belong to the same family, perhaps I had better entertain you next.

"I am called Cinnamon, and I'm just about as spicy as any of you. I am exactly as important to the pickled peaches as is Miss Clove, and where would the coffee cake be without me, I'd like to know?"

He paused and gazed about in a dramatic way that convulsed Jack, who whispered:

"Isn't he funny, Mother, so long and lank, and such an expression I never saw!"

"Did any of you ever hear of cinnamon

CINNAMON DOLL

candy?" continued the speaker. "Could it be cinnamon candy without me?"

As no one replied to this, he cried:

"Certainly not! and now I will show you where I grow. It is right here," and, with one stride of his long legs one foot rested on the Island of Ceylon in the Indian Ocean near Persia.

"Excuse me, Mr. Cinnamon, but where did you get your seven-league boots?" asked the Vinegar Cruet.

"They grew on me, so I didn't need to buy them. You can't tease me that way. I can't help it because I am long legged any more than you can help looking sour. When you turn sweet I'll have short legs; that's a bargain. Send me an invitation to your candy pull.

"Ladies and Gentlemen, please excuse this rude interruption, and I will proceed.

TALE OF THE

"When the cinnamon trees are almost two years old small branches are cut off and the outer bark removed, leaving the inner bark, which is then peeled off and dried.

"In drying it takes the form of rolls called quills, the smaller ones, as they dry, are thrust into the larger. Sometimes it is ground fine and packed in bags.

"I am not only used in flavouring food, but in many medicines.

"Now I think the spices have finished their tales, and we can have a complete change of programme."

"Oh!" cried Allspice, "before we go on let's have the Story Sprite again."

"Is it your desire that the Story Sprite appear?" asked Cinnamon Stick. "If so, Allspice and I will break this wishbone I see hanging over the hearth."

"Oh! Do! Do!" cried one and all.

"Very well, we will both wish for her to

CINNAMON DOLL

come, then we can't possibly fail whichever way it breaks."

And so snap went the bone, but much dismayed they were when it was found each held the short end, for the centre had taken to itself wings.

"Oh, I *wish* she would come anyhow!" they chorused, and once more from the flames sprang the Story Elf.

"You do not need to break wishbones to bring me. All that is necessary is just to *wish*, and here I am," she announced.

"This time I want to tell you more about a story you all know very well. It is called:

AND PIPED THOSE CHILDREN BACK AGAIN.

"Don't you love the Pied Piper story, and didn't your heart almost stop beating when the door in the mountain closed, shutting the children in?

AND PIPED THOSE

"And though you were glad one mother had her dear little boy left behind, no doubt your tears mingled with his as he limped alone down the mountain path trying in vain to comfort himself with the fleeting glimpse he had of that joyous country where the horses had wings and the bees no stings; where the birds were brighter than peacocks here and flowers of rare beauty grew in profusion.

"Can't you just see his beautiful, upturned, angel face? How could that great door close and leave *him* on the wrong side!

"But let me tell you a splendid fact. Sometimes the things that seem all wrong are the grandest things that ever happened, and true it is, though it may seem hard to believe, this little fellow was really on the right side of the door after all. And though he seemed shut out from the glad times awaiting them in that blissful land, just be-

CHILDREN BACK AGAIN

cause of this he was able to ring the joy bells of the village with his own hands because he was the only one there who could finally enter the magic door and carry the message that brought the children to their own again. And now I must tell you this beautiful thing that happened:

"After the little hamlet was bereft of her children the parents turned sadly back to their homes, while the muffled tones of the Pied Piper came no more to their ears.

"They could hardly believe it true. It must be a bad dream from which they would soon awaken.

"Many times a day the thrifty housewives stepped to their doors and listened in vain for the shrill baby voices to call to one another in their play.

"The wooden soldiers stood straight and stiff at their guns at 'Present arms!' waiting for the cry of 'Attention!' but no order was

AND PIPED THOSE

given—no sound of fife or drum disturbed the silence.

"The Dutch-faced dollies sat in corners, smiling so sweetly, waiting expectantly for their little mothers to rock them to sleep, but no lullabys came to their ears.

"The parents gazed at the various toys till their eyes were dim with tears and one night when the moon was big and round, and oh, so silvery, the Mayor tossed sleeplessly on his bed. Presently he arose, dressed, and crept out into the cool sweet night. His wife heard and followed.

"When they reached the street they found it peopled with many parents, waiting for they knew not what.

"The silvery light of the moon shed its glow upon the mountain, and as they looked, suddenly the portal opened wide, disclosing an inside gate of golden fretwork.

"Silently and slowly the portal swung

CHILDREN BACK AGAIN

back, and they whispered to one another, 'Was that the great door that shut the children in?'

"With bated breath they waited, and suddenly sweet strains of music filled the air.

" 'The Pied Piper!' cried the Mayor, with upraised hand.

"Never had they heard such notes, as clear and silvery as the moonbeams themselves. Then came the sound of children's voices, singing as never children sang, and though it was sweet it was so sad they could scarcely bear to listen, but it seemed to beckon them on.

"They hurried up the path taken by the children, and as they neared the door the words of the song amazed them, and drew forth exclamations.

" 'Keep your promise and we can come back!' was the burden of the song, and the Mayor cried:

AND PIPED THOSE

"'Come! The Piper must be told we are ready and eager to give him what we owe.'

"He led the way, but alas! they found the inside gate so small, only a child could enter. They called many times, but the only response was the sad little song of the children.

"'They cannot hear us. What will we do?' cried one mother on her knees before the gate, trying in vain to push her way through.

"'The lame boy, where is he?' queried the Mayor in anguished tones.

"'Fast asleep in his bed,' replied his mother.

"'Go quickly and bring him!' cried the Mayor. 'No one knows how soon the Portal may swing shut.'

"The father and mother hastened to the little home and to the crib where the boy lay

"The beauty of the scene almost overwhelmed him"

CHILDREN BACK AGAIN

sleeping sweetly, bathed in the glow of the silvery light.

" 'Come,' whispered the mother. 'Come.'

"The boy opened his eyes, sprang into his father's arms, and they hastened again up the mountain path.

" 'The door is open,' he cried joyously. 'Now I can have some one to play with!'

" 'I hope so,' breathed the mother. 'Go in and find the Piper. Tell him we beg of him to let us keep our promise. If he will only give us back our children we will give him all we have!'

"The little fellow limped through the golden portal and could go no farther, for the beauty of the scene almost overwhelmed him.

"Such flowers! Such trees, whose waving branches of tender green were filled with the most beautifully coloured birds he ever saw. Such shrubs, with glistening leaves flutter-

AND PIPED THOSE

ing timidly in the gentle breeze. Here the moon shone with a light that was never on land or sea.

"The boy gazed in raptures at the marvellous picture, then glanced keenly about for the Piper.

"Presently he saw him standing beneath an arched bower of twining roses, but so sad did he seem the boy hesitated to approach him.

"He took one step, then paused amazed. What had happened? He took another. Oh, joy of joys! He was lame no more! He dropped his crutch and ran. Ran as he had dreamed of running—just as other children did. Ran straight to the Piper.

"As the Piper clasped him in his arms, a heavenly smile lighted his face, and he cried:

"'At last they have heard the song. You can never know the joy you have brought to

CHILDREN BACK AGAIN

me this day. It was my anger that closed the gate and when it clanged to I said, "Never will I forgive them. Never." Ever since, the gate has been as though frozen shut. I knew why, but I wouldn't forgive.

" 'I did my best to make the children happy, but you see by their sad song, I failed. Have you noticed them?'

"The boy looked and for the first time really saw his playmates.

" 'What pretty clothes they have!' he exclaimed.

" 'Yes, the boys are clad in green and silver leaves. The girls' gowns are of flowers. Flowers such as grow only here. They may have a fresh gown every day, or oftener.'

" 'Where are their homes?' asked the boy.

" 'They live like the birds in the trees. Look!'

AND PIPED THOSE

"The boy gazed in wonder up into the tree tops, to see many tiny bowers woven of vines and flowers.

" 'Their beds are of rose petals, the wind rocks them to sleep, and the birds carol their lullaby. The humming birds hover over them as they dream. They drink honey with the bees. They eat luscious fruits such as one dreams of but never sees. With all of this they are not happy. They sigh for their dolls and soldiers, and weep for their parents.

" 'Lately I have felt my anger melting, and last night I suddenly knew I had forgiven all, and that instant the portal swung open. Soon I heard voices, but I could not move. Only a little child could break the spell. I am so thankful you could not follow with the others since only a child could pass through the golden gate to bring the message.'

CHILDREN BACK AGAIN

" 'Oh!' cried the boy in ecstasy. 'See! I can walk! I can run! I am so happy!'

" 'Yes,' said the Piper, 'I know. No one could be lame here now that the gate is open. This is the land of harmony; but tell me, boy, why did you come? Do tell me they sent you.'

" 'They did. They want to keep their promise.'

" 'They do? Will they give me the gold?' he asked eagerly.

" 'Oh, yes, they want to. They beg of you to take it.'

" 'Then tell them when the mountain path is paved with guilders I will bring the children.'

"The boy bounded away, but as he passed the children he was at once swept into the ring and in some mysterious way he also was clad in a garb of silvery leaves, while on his head was placed a crown of wondrous

AND PIPED THOSE

beauty, a crown of flowers which breathed forth a rare perfume.

"As they danced round and round, the song was no longer sad but rang out like joyous bells, filling the air with showers of gladness, while the Piper piped, and the birds twittered and trilled the gayest of tunes.

"They danced nearer and nearer the portal, and presently saw without, a sea of hungry faces and many outstretched arms.

"The boy shook himself loose and ran through the gate. With shining eyes he cried:

" 'See! I can walk! I can run! And I have more good news, but you must obey. Bring the gold quickly and you will soon have your children.'

"They rubbed their eyes and stared, then turned and ran down the mountain. Ran faster than the rats ever dreamed of running.

CHILDREN BACK AGAIN

Soon they came trooping up again each carrying a bag of gold.

" 'The Piper said when the path was paved with gold he would bring the children. Quick! I will help!' cried the boy.

"You should have seen them dropping the gold pieces in place, and in a twinkling the bags were empty and the road was one glittering ribbon.

"The boy ran through the portal to the Piper, crying: 'It is finished; come.'

"The Piper hurried to the entrance, looked down the shining path, paused, and waited. The silence was tense, while all gazed into his face wonderingly.

" 'The road is not finished,' he said gently. 'Look for yourselves. Some one has kept back gold that is still due. We will wait.'

"The Mayor flushed and knelt at his feet. 'It was I. I couldn't give quite all. Forgive me and I will bring more than enough.'

AND PIPED THOSE

"He strode down the path, soon to return carrying a leathern bag which clanked as he walked. At the feet of the Piper he shook out the golden circlets, which seemed bewitched as one after another rolled toward the empty spaces, where they spun round and round like so many golden tops, and finally settled into place. Those remaining piled themselves about the Piper's feet.

"The onlookers gazed in astonishment till suddenly they heard heavenly music. At once they stood either side of the golden pathway, watching the Piper followed by the children.

" 'All the little boys and girls,
With rosy cheeks and flaxen curls,
Tripping and skipping ran merrily after
The wonderful music with shouting and laughter.'

"On and on they went, their tiny feet treading silently the golden ribbon.

"The parents, with tears of joy streaming

CHILDREN BACK AGAIN

o'er their faces, followed, enraptured with the magic notes.

"Where the gleaming pathway ended the Piper paused, the parents embraced their little ones, then knelt at the feet of the Piper.

" 'Arise!' he cried in beseeching tones. 'I, too, am guilty. We have both made amends. Let us forget all wrongdoing and be happy. You have emptied your coffers but you are richer than ever.

" 'I do not want the gold. Let it lie a glittering pathway to the land of joy, where the children may dance and play to their hearts' content.

" 'As long as we do right the Golden Portal will never close. Farewell.'

"With these words he turned and walked toward the mountain door. The parents hurried to their homes, to find the boys ordering out the wooden soldiers, and the dolls drowsily smiling into mother eyes and listen-

MRS. SUGAR

ing to the far-away lullaby of the dear Pied Piper."

As the Story Elf finished she again vanished, and during the silence that followed the dolls thought they still heard the Piper's far away lullaby.

As it died away Allspice cried:

"How lovely to bring the children home again. I'm glad she told us about it, for I always felt sorry for the parents and the dear little lame boy all alone.

"I hope we can have her come again."

"Perhaps we may, but now we must go on with *our* stories.

"You know an old poem tells us little girls are made of sugar and spice and all things nice. Therefore, since Sugar is classed so closely with Spice, we might let that sweet lady talk to us for a while."

The fat Sugar Lady now came forward, and with a quick jerk of her skirts, showing

"Sometimes it is gingerbread, or maybe plump brown cookies"

her slippered feet, made an old-fashioned courtesy.

"Isn't she dear!" cried one and another, as they gazed admiringly at the quaint figure all dressed in white, which sparkled like frost on the window pane. Dainty bunches of rosebuds adorned her bonnet, and altogether she was a sweet picture.

"My dears," she cried, well aware of the admiration she excited.

"I know I am sweet as well as you do, but lest I become over-proud I will show you my real self growing, which really isn't anything to look at."

As she talked she untied her bonnet strings and untwisted one of the curls that bobbed about her snowy neck. The audience was startled to hear a squeak like the dying gasp of a rubber balloon.

As the squeak lingeringly died away, Sugar grew thinner and taller, and presently

MRS. SUGAR

there she was turned into a long yellow sugar cane.

A shout of laughter greeted this transformation, as Sugar Cane made an elaborate bow, beaming upon them as though delighted to see them.

"Allow me to make you acquainted with Mrs. Sugar's better half," he said.

"Butter half, you mean," shouted Vinegar.

"Throw in a little flour and a few eggs and we'll have a birthday cake."

"Which I would be delighted to do had I those useful ingredients."

"Ingredients?" said Cinnamon, thinking hard. "Will Little Salt, who is now peeping in the dictionary again, kindly let us know the meaning of that word?"

"It means a part of something," replied Salt, much dismayed that she had again been caught studying the big book when she should have been listening.

DOLL'S TALE

"Yes, a part of something; sugar, eggs and flour are a part of the cake. Now let us hear about this queer tall yellow stick."

"Very well, Sir. I come from a wild plant from India, Mexico, South America, and most tropical countries. They are here, and here, and here, and here," and in the twinkling of an eye he had walked about the globe and left his footprint in each place.

"I am also found in the red beet and yellow carrot. Perhaps it will be hard to believe, but this yellow cane, which is as sweet as honey, is placed between two large hard rollers until all the juice is squeezed out.

"This juice is boiled down, and when thick is poured off."

"Tut, tut, tut," gurgled the Molasses Jug; "don't step on my toes."

"Don't worry," laughed Sugar Cane. "I'm not going to tell any more of your story.

MRS. SUGAR

I had to tell that much to get at what settles to the bottom, which is my sweet wife.

"It is first brown sugar. That is purified by filtration, and when clear white takes the various names of loaf sugar, lump sugar, and refined sugar, according to the degree of purification.

"Refined sugar is the pulverised confectioners' sugar and is used in candies.

"Granulated sugar is made by stirring while the strong syrup crystallises and forms small grains or crystals.

"While I know I am not very pretty, yet the children in the warm countries love me dearly. They clamour for a piece of sugar cane to suck, just as the children here beg for candy sticks. Some of the poor little ones have nothing to eat all day long but a stick of sugar cane, and nowhere to sleep but on a door step. They run around in bare feet and with scarcely any clothes!"

DOLL'S TALE

"Here! Here!" came the smothered tones of Mrs. Sugar. "You have told the whole story. I think you shouldn't wind up by making everybody weep. Blow yourself up and let me come forth once more, please."

Then Sugar Cane began to dwindle as a gust of wind blew through his pipes. Shorter and fatter he grew, till behold, there was dear Mrs. Sugar, smiling down at them as she again tied her bonnet strings.

"I never did see such a man. So dismal as he grows sometimes. What if the children do only have sugar cane all day. It's good and makes them fat, and a jollier lot I never saw. They love to go barefooted; and as for clothes, who wants any where the weather is boiling hot all the time?

"Don't waste any tears on him any of you. Let's hear from Molasses. She will send your tears flying as high as a kite."

At this summons the Molasses Jug now appeared. Her gown was a beautiful shade of golden brown, with touches of sunshiny yellow here and there. She really wasn't a jug, but looked like one from the fact that she kept her arm crooked up just like a jug handle.

"Well," she said gaily. "Mr. Sugar pretty near told you my story, I stopped him just in time. I come in just where the juice from the sugar cane boils down thick. That was my own splendid self that was poured off.

"I love the time when I gurgle down into a barrel, and fairly hug myself when that barrel is in a grocery store waiting to be sold. I always wonder what kind of a home I am going to, and what will be done with me.

"I sit there in the dark, and presently the spigot in the barrel is turned, and the thick stream gurgles into jugs. The jugs are placed in a grocery wagon. The driver

MOLASSES DOLL

whistles a merry tune, and away we go into so many homes.

"I make so many good things, and it is such fun guessing what I'm going to be in each time. Sometimes it is gingerbread, or may be plump brown cookies. Again, it is pudding with fat plums swelling up inside.

"Once a grand thing happened. It was the day before Christmas. The driver was hurrying the horse along at the very edge of town.

"Suddenly something startled the horse, and he ran away. The wagon overturned. Everything was thrown about in the snow. My jug broke and I began to run out all over. I had good company though, for popcorn, cranberries, and all sorts of things were scattered about me.

"The grocery boy gathered up most of the stuff and away he went. I was hopeless, and thought what a miserable Christmas I was to have. No good to anybody. Suddenly I pricked up my ears. Children were crying, and I heard one say:

" 'Can't have any Christmas at all. Not a speck of anything. No money to buy anything with!'

"A group of them were trudging through the snow from school. When they saw me one said: 'What's that?'

"Wasn't I glad I was molasses. Most anything else would have been of no use at such a time. I could hardly keep still when I saw one after another poke a finger into the brown mass and taste.

" 'Molasses!' they cried in one breath.

"With a whoop of delight they ran into a nearby home, and came back with a pail and cups. The snow had a glassy crust and I hadn't sunken in at all. So all they had to do was to scoop, and there I was. They

MOLASSES DOLL

scooped and scraped till they had a good pail full.

"I saw a few ears of popcorn that had lodged down in a little hollow, so I let a small stream run after them. The children spied them, and such a shout went up as you never heard! Luckily the snow was fresh fallen and clean, so they really had made quite a find.

"We were hurried into the house, and when the mother and father came home from their work, looking sad enough because they could not give the children any Christmas, they were greeted with the cries of 'Merry Christmas! Merry Christmas!'

"It would have done your hearts good to have seen that candy pull, and the pop corn balls were the finest ever made. They had a perfectly good Christmas that didn't cost a cent.

TALE OF THE

"So I think molasses is quite important in this world even if it is cheap."

Molasses sat down amid a round of applause.

"What a nice story! I wish some one would tell another," murmured little Allspice, whose earnest blue eyes and clasped hands showed how she had loved the story.

"A splendid idea! The night is slowly passing; perhaps some of us may think up some interesting stories; incidents we have seen in our various home lands.

"Now let's hear from the Vinegar King. We have had much sweet, perhaps we would like a little sour for a change."

His Majesty was tall and thin, dressed in velvet knee breeches and fancy coat with silver trimmings. His cockade hat looked as though he really did belong to royalty, but so sour an expression did he wear you could tell at once that he stood for nothing sweet.

"Suddenly something startled the horse, and he ran away"

VINEGAR KING

"Ladies and Gentlemen: I am happy—"

"Happy—you?" queried the audience in gales of laughter.

"I didn't mean to say I was happy. I started to say I am happy to inform you that in wine countries I come from fermented poor wines, elsewhere from malt or apple cider."

With that he sat down.

"Here! Here! Is that all you have to tell us?" cried Cinnamon Stick.

"All! It is much more than Molasses had to say."

"You have talked for twenty seconds. Molasses entertained us for many minutes!"

"Yes, Mr. Chairman, but if you simmer down what Molasses told you of her history, it will take three seconds by the clock to say it. It was this: 'I am the juice from the sugar cane boiled down and gurgled into a barrel!'"

TALE OF THE

Vinegar tried so hard to imitate Molasses, even to the sweet expression, he sat down amid roars of laughter.

Molasses now hopped up in the greatest haste, crying:

"So I did gurgle into a barrel, and into a jug, too. It was all there was to tell. Sugar Cane had to tell the beginning of me because we came from the same thing. It was why I told the story, and dear knows it was a sweet story."

"The gentleman with silver trimmed knee breeches will kindly tell us something further of himself," said Cinnamon Stick in bland tones. "What are you good for?"

"I am used for soothing remedies in the pharmacies."

"Soothing!" laughted Salt and Pepper. "I hope you have your picture on the outside of the bottles."

"I do. They especially asked for it. I am

VINEGAR KING

good for many things besides medicine. Sour pickles could never be made without me, and as for peach pickles, you might have all the cloves and cinnamon in the world in them, would they be at all if it were not for me? As for my looks, I can't help them. We all have to look like we are, and even though I look and seem sour, at heart I am sweet because really I have to have sugar to make the mother."

"Mother!" cried bashful Allspice. "Have you really a dear mother?"

"Oh, my dear, not that kind of a mother. It is just some thick stringy stuff that grows in vinegar as it ferments and makes it ferment quicker. It is just called mother.

"That is all I know about me. Thank you for your kind attention."

"You are very welcome," said Cinnamon Stick. "You really did very well after all.

TALE OF THE

"Now let's hear from Miss Citron. She sounds very sweet and good."

"And I am sweet and good, too," said the doll with the large green head, gorgeously gowned in purple.

"I grow in Spain." Here she sat down on the top of the globe and rolled over and over till she reached that spot where she was to be found, then rose and continued:

"My tree has an upright smooth trunk with a branchy head rising from five to fifteen feet, adorned with large oval spear-shaped leaves. See, my hat is made of one. Isn't it *chic?*" and she placed the odd hat on her head and paraded about for a moment.

"Don't mistake me for a Pathé Moving Picture fashion show, please, for I never aspired to anything higher than fruit cake and pastries.

"My fruit is different from the lemon in that it has no knob at the top and the rind is

CITRON DOLL

much thicker. My tree has purple blossoms that are white inside. The seeds of the fruit are bitter. After they are taken out I am cut in half and dried in sugar and make a delicious confection.

"I am sorry my story is short, but that is really all there is to tell."

"Very good, indeed, and now we will hear from the ballet girls, Orange and Lemon, who seem in a flutter to tell their tales," announced Mr. Cinnamon Stick.

The Orange and Lemon Dolls now came forward, and after a sweeping bow danced like fairies about the hearth, their orange and yellow skirts fluffing about their tiny feet.

"Opera glasses! Opera glasses!" shouted one.

"All music and words of the opera here," sang another.

"Standing room only," cried another.

TALES OF THE ORANGE

Mr. Cinnamon Stick bade them be quiet, and Orange began her story.

"We come from about the same parts of the world; watch and you will see where."

The eyes of the audience followed the pair as they heeled and toed over the globe, touching daintily Italy, Spain, Portugal, Florida, and California.

"The California orange is liked best because it has no seeds. It is a deep orange colour with a thick skin.

"The Florida orange is a shade lighter and has a thinner skin.

"We also grow in Mexico—here—but the Mexican orange cannot be shipped because it will not keep. It is sweet and delicious, however, and much loved by the natives.

"One wonderful thing about the orange tree is that at the same time, on the same tree, you will find the buds, blossoms, the

AND LEMON DOLLS

green and ripe fruit, because they grow slowly. Also the grape fruit is sometimes grafted on our trees. There are oranges that will hang on the trees for two years, so they can be picked at any time, which is most convenient.

"The trees stand about twenty-three feet apart and must not be chilled for it hurts the buds. When a cold snap comes, the owners build fires here and there in the orange groves and keep them all snug and warm. They must watch the weather reports very closely, as in a short time the cold might ruin the orange crop.

"One thousand oranges have been taken from one tree. When the tree is no longer fruitful, its hard, fine-grained, yellowish wood is valued for inlaid work.

"The orange was first found in India, then spread to Western Asia, Spain, Italy, and is now grown in all tropical lands.

TALES OF THE ORANGE

"Now, Lemon may tell us about herself, as that is all I know."

"I also am from Spain, and all those countries we touched," said the Lemon Doll.

"I grew on a tree with three thousand in the family.

"We are picked green because then we keep better and the skins are thinner. If we are left in our tree house until grown to full size our skins are thick, and we are sent to England, where we are sugared and dried and named sugared lemon peel.

"We don't sound like much, but when you see us in heaps and piles in the groceries, and see the lot of money we bring in to the owners, you find we are quite worth while, for we are shipped all over the world, and wherever you are you will usually find us on the table, if you find no other fruit."

"Right you are, my dears. You are both a most important food, and we are glad

AND LEMON DOLLS

we met up with you," cried Cinnamon Stick.

"And now *I'm* going to wish again for the Story Sprite. I want a Christmas story."

"Oh, joy!" exclaimed the audience, rapturously beaming upon the Story Sprite, who sprang from the back log at the magic word "wish," singing gaily:

"And a Christmas story you shall have. Here is my favourite one. It is called

ANNA BELLE'S CHRISTMAS EVE.

"Anna Belle had had a very exciting day, and now, curled up on the window seat, her head pillowed on downy cushions, she sat watching the sleighs flying by.

"It was a glorious night. The moon shed its silvery glow on the busy scene, and Anna Belle drowsily noted the people passing with arms filled and pockets bulging.

" 'I wish I could see what's in those packages,' she murmured. 'I think Christmas is queer anyhow.'

" 'Why?' came in tinkling tones to her ears.

"Anna Belle jumped, for there beside her was a beautiful fairy, holding on high a silver wand, on the end of which gleamed a star.

" 'Why?' persisted the fairy creature, determined to have an explanation of such a statement.

" 'Well, I ask for a lot of things I never get, and I get a lot of things I don't want.'

" 'You do?' said the Fairy inquiringly.

" 'Yes, every year I do. In the attic are boxes and boxes of things I didn't care at all for. Somehow I'm never very happy at Christmas time.'

" 'Are you *giving* any presents this year?'

" 'Oh, yes, Papa always gives me money to buy them, but I didn't spend it all. I've

CHRISTMAS EVE

asked for a bracelet, and if I don't get it I'm going to buy one with what I have left.'

"The fairy glanced about the beautiful room, where seemed to be everything to make one happy, then she gently asked:

"'Are the gifts you bought gifts you feel sure are wanted by those who will receive them?'

"Anna Belle flushed as she tossed her curls and replied:

"'Perhaps not. Papa always says, "You can't get something for nothing," and you see I didn't want to spend all my money.'

"'Did you have a happy time buying these gifts?'

"'Well, no. Do you think any one is *very* happy at Christmas time?'

"'That depends. Some are very, very happy.'

"'Yes, I know. People with bushels of

gifts are, especially if they are really what they want.'

" 'Oh,' laughed the Fairy. 'I know people who have scarcely any money to buy presents and yet are having a lovely Christmas with presents made out of nothing. People who are as poor as crows, and yet are bubbling over with joy this very night.'

"Anna Belle opened her eyes very wide at this statement.

" 'Making a Christmas out of nothing, and as poor as crows!' she echoed. 'Just how poor is that? I'd like to see them.'

" 'You would? Come with me then,' and after a wave of the silvery wand Anna Belle found herself floating along in mid air like a bird.

" 'Oh!' she cried. 'What fun! I wish I could always be a fairy!'

" 'If you wish it hard enough you may be. Now follow me very closely for we aren't the

"She was making dolls from bottles"

CHRISTMAS EVE

only fairies abroad Christmas Eve. The air is full of them.'

"Anna Belle looked about her, and sure enough, it was almost like June bug season. She felt them whizzing past her, and at times their whirring wings fairly brushed her cheeks.

" 'Oh, how lovely it is!' she exclaimed. 'How different it all looks from above!'

" 'Yes, dear, everything looks different from above. Do you see that wee brown house far over in that meadow, all alone?'

" 'Yes,' replied Anna Belle; 'are they poor as crows?'

" 'Poorer, they haven't even any feathers,' laughed the Fairy, as they gently floated down, down, till they could peer into a window of the little house.

"A mother sat by a table sewing. Anna Belle watched to see that she was making dolls from bottles.

ANNA BELLE'S

"She fashioned heads by placing a wad of cotton in a piece of muslin. Giving the cloth a twist, she had a perfect round ball which she shaped and tied down over a cork. On this she skilfully painted a face, then tied a trim little bonnet about it, and behold, there was a smiling bit of a creature awaiting the next move.

"She then made petticoat, dress and coat, and stood it in a corner while she made another. As she worked she smiled so sweetly the whole room seemed aglow.

"'Come and see who will have these gifts,' whispered the Fairy.

"Anna Belle followed and peeped in another window. There she saw a number of little children all snuggled up fast asleep.

"'Look!' whispered the Fairy, and pointed to a stand where were a few gifts. A pincushion made of bits of ribbon from a scrap bag, and a workbox made from a cigar box.

CHRISTMAS EVE

This was a work of art indeed. Pockets had been tacked inside, and on the bottom of the box lay a spool of thread.

" 'Looks lonesome, doesn't it?' whispered the Fairy.

"Anna Belle nodded as she thought of her own beautiful workbox of carved ivory with gold thimble and all sorts of beautiful fittings.

"Then she remembered another laid away in the attic, one of the things she didn't want.

"These two crude gifts were marked in childish hand, 'For Mother with much love.'

" 'Love is sticking out all over those things,' said the Fairy. 'Come down and see how she is getting on with her bottle family.'

"They went below, to find the dolls nearly finished, and a fine ready-made family it was.

"Father, mother, children, and even a weenty teenty pill bottle doll, dressed as a

ANNA BELLE'S

baby in long clothes, was pinned to the mother, the tiny head nestled close to the spot where her heart should be.

"'They are lovely!' declared Anna Belle.

"'They are, indeed, and they can do what many of the finest dolls you buy cannot. They can stand and you can have great fun with them.'

"'I'm going to make some,' said Anna Belle. 'I think they are cute. What is she doing now?'

"'Why, don't you see? Some one has given her a branch from a Christmas tree. She is fastening the dolls to it. Now she's poking the coals, she's going to pop corn and string it for the tree. That cost one penny. She's also going to make molasses candy. See it bubbling in that kettle? Molasses is very cheap and it will be the only candy they will have, but they will be wild over it, just because only at Christmas time they have it.

CHRISTMAS EVE

" 'Now come and I'll show you crow number two.'

"Anna Belle was loath to leave this interesting window, but she obediently followed on.

" 'Look in here,' whispered the Fairy, as they paused by another humble home.

"Anna Belle looked, to see an empty stocking swinging from the mantel. On it was pinned a paper, and Anna Belle read the large printed words:

"Dear Santa Claus—If you have enough things to go round won't you give my sister a music box and a readin' buck. She's lame and can't play like me. You needn't give me anything. I can hear the music and read her's.   "JAMIE."

"Anna Belle's eyes filled as she read, and followed the Fairy to see two children fast asleep, dreaming of what they hoped they might find in the morning.

" 'They have no mother. The father isn't

much good, but does his best to feed them. In the morning those stockings will be as empty as they are now.'

"'Dear! Dear! Why doesn't some one know about it?' asked Anna Belle tearfully.

"'Some one does know now,' replied the Fairy with a wise nod as they floated on.

"'I hope they'll do something then,' said Anna Belle.

"'I hope so,' whispered the Fairy. 'Look in here,' and Anna Belle peered in a window.

"Here a child of perhaps twelve or fourteen was seated at a table, working busily. Anna Belle watched to see her making paper dolls. She cut them out, painted faces and hair, then made a number of cunning dresses, coats and hats, placed them in envelopes and marked the outside.

"They watched till she had three ready, then slipped them into the stockings, hanging waiting.

CHRISTMAS EVE

"The love light in her eyes was sweet to behold and as she stood over the lamp to put it out, Anna Belle noticed the rare delicate beauty of her face.

"When all was dark the Fairy moved on.

" 'She didn't even hang up her own stocking,' said Anna Belle.

" 'No one to fill it. She mothers those three little ones, and it's all she can do to make things go, but did you ever see any one look happier? See the card on this door knob?'

"Anna Belle paused to read:

"Dear Santa—Please bring me a sleeping doll. Even if you can't spare one, if you would just let me hold one a moment and sing it to sleep once I will be glad. I am a good girl.

"Elsie."

" 'See her! Isn't she dear?' cried Anna Belle, as she peeped in the window to see a beautiful plump little girl fast asleep.

ANNA BELLE'S

" 'She looks like a sleeping doll herself. Will she get the doll, do you think?'

" 'I hope so. It all depends,' said the Fairy.

"They floated along for some time, and presently went down to hover over some children looking in the window of a toy store.

"Wistful little faces they had, and their clothes told Anna Belle they must get their fun out of just looking.

"Farther on in front of the candy store huddled a shabby crowd, gazing at the sparkling goodies.

" 'Come away, please, I don't want to see any more. Surely they aren't happy,' cried Anna Belle.

" 'They are as happy as they can be. Each one of them had a penny in a tightly closed fist, wondering what to buy to take home and put in an empty stocking.

" 'Let's stop here a moment,' whispered the

CHRISTMAS EVE

Fairy, poising on the top of a Christmas tree in front of a big store.

"Anna Belle, standing beside her, noticed that as she held on high her wand the star shone out so bright and beautiful the people below paused and gazed in wonder. The happy faces beamed even brighter and the unhappy ones changed instantly.

" 'What does it mean?' whispered one and another, while one little girl cried:

" 'Why, Mother, it's *the* Star. Don't you know?'

" 'Yes,' whispered the mother, clasping more closely the little hand and passing on.

" 'What made the cross ones look so glad, and the happy ones look more so?' asked Anna Belle, as she watched the throngs below.

" 'Don't you know really?' asked the Fairy.

"Anna Belle pondered a while, then looked

at the sky to see it thickly dotted with stars, and saw that One shone more brightly than any of the others. She then turned to look at the star on the end of the wand, but behold, it had vanished.

" 'Where is it?' she asked in surprise.

" 'It came down and did its work and then went back where it belongs,' replied the Fairy with a roguish twinkle, and Anna Belle stared for a moment at the splendid bright star, then said softly:

" 'I understand it now, and why it could do it, but I had forgotten what Christmas really means.

" 'For a long time it has seemed to mean only things. Gifts, and not only gifts, but certain kinds of gifts.

" 'Oh!' she said wistfully, 'I wish I could do something to help. Was that what you meant when you kept saying, "That depends"?'

CHRISTMAS EVE

" 'That was just what I meant. Now you have seen the Star, and I know all will be well.'

"Anna Belle seemed busily thinking, and the Fairy waited.

" 'The attic is full of presents I didn't want, and I have a lot of money I was going to use for the bracelet.'

" '*If* you didn't get it,' laughed the Fairy.

" 'I don't want it now. I'd rather use it for these poor little children. Elsie must have a doll. I have one, and a music box, and many "Readin' " books with pictures, but how can we get them to the places?'

" 'Fairies are stronger than you think. I will summon my helpers.'

"Anna Belle then heard a sound as of wind whistling around the corners. In a moment there appeared fairies without number. Such silvery sprites they were Anna Belle longed to take one to her heart and keep for ever and ever.

"'Come!' cried the Fairy, who seemed to be the leader.

"As she floated away all followed, and Anna Belle found they were headed straight for her own home and the attic.

"As she wondered how they would get in, she found herself flying easily through the tiny bird window high up in the tower.

"'How lovely!' she cried. 'I never knew it was for fairies!'

"'Show what we are to take,' cried the Fairy. 'We must hurry.'

"Anna Belle pointed out a music box, books, dishes, balls, skates. In fact, toys of every description. Then she opened one large box to find a beautiful doll with eyes closed in slumber. 'For Elsie,' she whispered, and watched to see each fairy gather up a gift and press close to its shining bosom.

"'Show what we are to take,' cried the Fairy. 'We must hurry'"

CHRISTMAS EVE

"'Are we really going to take them?' she asked.

"'We wouldn't miss the joy of it for anything,' replied her fairy friend.

"They floated away, Anna Belle holding to her heart the sleeping doll. She tried to recall why she hadn't wanted it, for it was so pretty. Then she flushed, for she remembered that she had been cross over this very doll because she had asked for a brown-eyed doll and this one had blue eyes!

"'I didn't deserve any doll, nor anything,' she said. 'I didn't know I was so bad.'

"'Forget it!' laughed the Fairy. 'We can't afford to be thinking over our wrong-doings. If we have started on the right track we will have enough to do to keep within it.

"'Here is the candy store. I know you want some. Give me your money; I'll get it for you. I know the man well. He'll double what he gives me, for he well knows what I'll do with it.'

"In some mysterious way Anna Belle found in a moment each one was carrying a basket of bonbons on a tiny arm as they floated on.

" 'Here is Elsie,' whispered the Fairy presently.

"Anna Belle placed the doll in Elsie's arms, then filled the stockings with other toys and sweets. In the toe she placed a shining gold piece.

"The music box, books, and other toys were left in the home of the lame child; also a gold piece shone in the toe of each stocking hanging there.

"The paper doll girl was generously remembered, and the bottle dolls smiled gratefully at the load of gifts left at their feet.

"Anna Belle's eyes shone as she thought of

CHRISTMAS EVE

the joy this Christmas was to bring to so many hearts.

"'How many?' asked the Fairy, who seemed to know what she was thinking.

"Anna Belle pondered as they floated homeward. Presently she cried: 'Why, just think, it's twenty-four!'

"'Only twenty-four? I counted twenty-five.'

"Again Anna Belle went over them, then said: 'I can't remember the odd one.'

"The Fairy sent forth a bubbling, rippling laugh, which puzzled Anna Belle for a moment, then she twinkled and cried:

"'Why, I'm the odd one. I never was so happy. When did it begin? Oh, I know; it was when I saw the Star, wasn't it?'

"'Yes, indeed,' replied the Fairy, 'and not only when you saw the Star, but when you remembered the meaning of it.

"'The love that came in with the Christ

Child and His spirit of loving and giving, not only of gifts but of Himself, has come down with the ages, and will go on and on.'

" 'I'm so glad I found it out. I really don't care now whether I get the bracelet, or not,' declared Anna Belle, as they floated into her bedroom window.

" 'No, but see!' and the Fairy pointed with her wand, on the end of which Anna Belle again saw the shining Star sending a glow of light over her dresser, and there lying on its velvet bed she beheld a beautiful circlet of dull gold.

"Much excited, she whispered: 'Is it plain? I really wanted it jewelled.' Then she laughed and added: 'No, I don't care how it is. Just so it's a bracelet, for I'm afraid I do kind of want it. Is it wrong to want it? If it is, I'll try till I don't.'

"The Fairy gently caressed her, then

CHRISTMAS EVE

touched the golden circlet with her wand.

" 'No, it isn't wrong to want it now that you remember the true meaning of Christmas, and want to keep it with the true Christmas spirit. See!'

"Anna Belle looked to see a starry jewel embedded in the gold, then she noticed the Star had vanished from the wand.

"She looked quickly out at the sky, where the steady light of the Star shone straight into her eyes.

" 'I'm glad you didn't take that Star,' she whispered. 'We couldn't get along without it.'

" 'My, no. I couldn't take that Star. That's the Star of Bethlehem, you know. This is just a weenty teenty shadow of that Star, that's why it isn't quite so bright.'

" 'It's bright enough for me, and means a lot. How can I ever thank you for this night's work?' asked Anna Belle.

ANNA BELLE'S

"'Never again lose sight of the Star and I will be more than repaid. Good-bye.'

"Anna Belle watched her out of sight, then turned and—dear me! she opened her eyes; the sleighs were still flying past, for she could hear the bells ringing so merrily.

"'How much sweeter they sound,' she cried. 'They seem to be saying, "Merry Christmas! Merry Christmas!" I wonder why I didn't notice it before.'

"She ran down-stairs to find Mother busily wrapping packages. She looked at Anna Belle and cried:

"'Why, child, what makes your eyes so bright, and why do you look so glad? I heard you saying all sorts of things as you slept.'

"'Oh, Mother! If you only knew,' and thereupon she told the whole story of her dream, omitting the part about the bracelet. When she had finished she drew her mother

CHRISTMAS EVE

to the window, where together they gazed at the Star.

"Mother's eyes were full of tears, as she said gently, 'Ring the bell, dear.'

"The maid appeared, and Mother asked that John bring out the double sleigh at once, adding:

"'Then come to me; bring Annie also. We have work to do.'

"Wonderingly the maids followed to the attic and brought down many boxes lying there, waiting for they knew not what.

"'Help me to tie them up separately in white tissue paper. Use the prettiest ribbons.'

"They worked busily, and soon a more Christmasy lot of bundles it would be hard to find.

"They placed them in baskets, together with warm clothes, beautiful dresses of Anna Belle's that were hardly worn.

ANNA BELLE'S

"Presently Anna Belle, Mother, and the baskets were packed in the big sleigh, dashing down the street.

"One stop they made, at the candy store, then on they went.

" 'Do you think you can find Elsie, and the little lame girl, and the house where the bottle dolls are?'

" 'I'm sure I can,' replied Mother. 'I happen to know them all.'

"And find them they did, and many others who were not in the dream.

" 'Oh, Mother! isn't it sweet to do?' cried Anna Belle, her bright eyes shining up at the Star.

" 'It is, indeed, dear. I'm very glad you had the dream, for I fear I also was forgetting the real meaning of Christmas and almost entirely losing sight of the Star.'

"She held the child close till the joy ride was over, then kissed her, saying:

CHRISTMAS EVE

"'I don't know when I have been so happy!'

"'Nor I, Mother dear; and we owe it all to the Good Fairy.'

"'We do, indeed. May she never cease to wave her starry wand. Good night, my child, good night.'

"Soon Anna Belle slept, and as she slept the starlight beamed on her sweet face, and presently it shone also on a golden circlet lying on its velvet pillow on the dresser.

"The dream seemed really coming true, for there embedded in the gold gleamed a starry jewel.

"When Anna Belle found it the next morning, she ran to Mother's room crying earnestly:

"'Mother, *do* you think the Fairy left it?'

"'No doubt,' replied Mother with twinkling eyes, 'at least she must have touched it with her wand, for you see she has left her messenger:

" 'and the Star is shining.' "

The story ended, the Sprite vanished, and in her place the light of a beautiful star shed a halo about the little heads.

The tiny creatures sat spellbound, dreaming again with Anna Belle, till they were suddenly awakened by Cinnamon Stick who cried:

"Well! Well! Wasn't that a grand Christmas story! I almost felt as though we too were flying fairies playing Santa Claus, but since we are just plain mince pie elves playing school we better go on with our game.

"Now I am most anxious to hear from the black and white pair of twins. Allow me to introduce Salt and Pepper, both of whom seem very necessary in this world of ours."

"I am used very extensively as an April Fool"

AND PEPPER TWINS

Salt and Pepper now teetered forward. A cute little pair, indeed. Salt, all robed in frosty white, first began, and saucily cried out her big name of Sodium Chloride.

"I haven't much to say except that I look so like sugar you can hardly tell which is which. For that reason I am used very extensively as an April Fool and am most popular on that day.

"I come principally from the United States, of which you all know without my showing you; from Michigan, New York, Ohio, Louisiana, West Virginia, California, Kansas, and Utah.

"Michigan and New York gave in 1888 about three quarters of all the salt produced in the United States.

"The salt of California is made by evaporation of sea water. That of Utah from water of Great Salt Lake.

TALES OF THE SALT

"That found in Louisiana and Kansas comes by mining rock salt.

"I'll give you a riddle. What is it that has to be in most everything we eat, or else it isn't good? I'll answer because you couldn't possibly guess. It's salt.

"You could hardly enjoy a meal without me. What would a table be without the salt box? And as for birthday parties, they just couldn't have them if I vanished from the earth."

"'Tisn't true," cried Orange. "A party I was at once was almost ruined because of you. You worked into the ice cream, and what's a party without ice cream? No one could eat it and the children cried!"

"That's true," said Salt. "I forgot to tell you that while a little of me is most necessary, too much of a good thing is worse than nothing.

AND PEPPER TWINS

"Now my twin brother will tell you of himself."

Black Pepper, dressed in a black velvet suit and cap, politely bowed as he removed his hat.

"Kechoo! Kechoo!" sneezed the audience.

"Put your cap on quickly," whispered Salt; "don't you see you are making them sneeze?"

"Oh, pardon me!" apologised Pepper. "I didn't think that politeness would cause such distress. My story is very short.

"I come from all damp tropical countries, and my tree is a joy to behold, when hanging full of scarlet berries against the background of green leaves. The spikes are gathered when the berries begin to turn red. The berries are rubbed off and dried and form then the ordinary black pepper.

TALE OF THE

"The white pepper consists of the seeds of the same fruit allowed to ripen and deprived of their pulp. The white pepper finds its largest market in China, which is right here.

"There is a plant of the genus Capsicum. From those pods come Cayenne or red pepper.

"That's all," he cried, with a funny quick bow.

"Your stories are short, but you are both about as necessary an article of food as I know of," said Mr. Cinnamon Stick, "and now let us hear from this apple-cheeked maid, all about her lovely fruit, the Apple."

The Apple-faced Doll tripped forward in the greatest of haste.

"I shall sit while I talk," she said, seating herself and smoothing out her snowy apron. "I have a long story to tell which, I am sure, you will all love."

APPLE DOLL

"A story! A story!" rippled through the audience, as the dolls crept close to the speaker, and with clasped hands awaited this treat.

Little Allspice placed herself in the rosy-cheeked maiden's lap, and a pretty picture it was to see her upturned face in the golden gleam of the dancing flames.

"Well," began the maid with the jolly smile, "the apple is to be found most everywhere in mild climates. It first came from Avella, a town in Campania, right there." As she spoke she pointed with a long pointer standing near by, to a place in Italy.

"It was introduced into America from England in 1629 by the Governor of Massachusetts Bay.

"There are many varieties of apples, sweet and sour, hard and soft, eating and cooking apples.

"The cider in the mincemeat is made from

the juice of the apples. They are crushed in a cider mill and the juice is strained. Some apples would delight a child's heart with their beautiful colours of gold and crimson, and some grow to an enormous size.

"And now for the story:

"Once there was a man who was very, very poor. He had been a farmer and no one raised such fine crops as did he. By and by, in some way, he lost his farm and was left all alone.

"He had always wanted to do some grand thing, something that would make many people happy, but what could he do? He had no money. All he had was a small boat.

"As he trudged along one day he saw some old sacks lying under a tree. As he looked at them he had a splendid thought. A thought that seemed to have wings and came flying from far away. Oh, it was a beautiful

JOHNNY APPLESEED

thought, and seemed to be singing a little song in his heart as he picked up the sacks and placed them in his boat, jumped in himself and floated away.

"As he rowed down the stream the man watched the shore with keen eyes. When he saw an apple orchard he rowed to land, tied his boat, hastened to the homes near the orchards and asked for work.

"He cut wood, carried water, and did all sorts of odd chores. In payment for this work he asked for food, and what else do you suppose?

"The people were so surprised at what he asked for they could hardly believe him. He asked that he might have the seeds from the apples on the ground under the trees— only the seeds.

"Of course they gladly gave him such a simple thing, and as he cut the fruit the neighbour children swarmed about him.

THE STORY OF

"From one place to another he went, always adding to his store of seeds.

"Some generous farmers gave him also cuttings of peach, pear, and plum trees, and grape vines.

"Day after day, day after day, he cut up the fruit, while the children sat at his feet and listened to thrilling tales of what he had seen in his travels. Of the Indians with their gay blankets and feathers, of their camps where they lived in the forests.

"Of their dances and war paint; their many coloured, beaded necklaces and jingling, silver chains and bracelets. Of their beady-eyed babies strapped to boards.

"Of the wolves which came out at night to watch him as he sat by his fire; of the beautiful deer who ran across his path.

"He sang funny songs for the children and taught them all sorts of games.

"When it came time to go on, they begged

"The children sat at his feet and listened to thrilling tales"

JOHNNY APPLESEED

him to stay. Never before had they been so amused, but on he went, and when his bags were full, and he had a goodly store of food, he started on to carry out the splendid thought. Oh, it was a grand thing he was going to do.

"The little boat went on and on, till houses were no more to be seen. Splendid forests lined the banks here and there. Then he paused, for this was what he was seeking— a place where no one lived.

"He landed and went about with a bag of seeds, and when he reached an open place in a forest he planted seeds and cuttings of the trees and vines; then wove a brush fence about them to keep the deer away. He then hastened back to his boat and drifted on.

"In many, many places he landed and planted seeds, and all the orchards of the Ohio and Mississippi Valley we owe to this man.

THE STORY OF

"Years after when settlers came looking for a place to live they chose these spots where, to their great surprise, they found all sorts of trees loaded with fruit.

"This man's name was John Chapman, but he was nicknamed Johnny Appleseed.

"The settlers were glad indeed when he appeared and told them the orchards were the fruit of his labours, and they were all eager to entertain him.

"And so he ended his life in this land of fruit and plenty.

"I must tell you a story of one certain little tree.

"In one of the houses of the settlement where Johnny Appleseed loved to stay there lived a dear little boy, just a wee toddler, named Jack.

"Dearly did the child love to follow the old man about as he worked, for Johnny Ap-

JOHNNY APPLESEED

pleseed's work was by no means finished when the trees were bearing fruit.

"Those trees had to be pruned; that meant all the dead branches had to be cut off. In the spring the blossoms had to be sprayed to keep the bugs out of the cores of the fruit; the trunk had to be watched to see that it was not marred in any way, as a small gash might mean the loss of the tree in time.

"One day Johnny, with little Jack, went to the village post office, and there found a letter and a package.

"It was the child's birthday, and he was most interested in the small parcel thinking it might be for him.

" 'Jack,' cried Johnny after reading the letter, 'what do you s'pose is in it? Look!' and he disclosed a mass of brown glossy seeds. 'The letter says they are from a wonderful new kind of apple. How would you

THE STORY OF

like an apple tree all your own for a birthday present?'

" 'Yeth,' lisped Jack, 'an apple tree all my own.'

" 'Then let's pretend you are another Johnny Appleseed, starting an orchard. Bring your cart.'

"Jack's eyes shone at the word 'pretend,' for he dearly loved it, and soon came drawing the little red cart, in which Johnny placed the package of seeds.

" 'Now we'll go and get a lunch,' said the old man as they walked to the kitchen door.

"Jack rapped on the door, and Mother appeared.

" 'If you please, Marm,' said Johnny, 'we are going on an expedition. We have a birthday and we want to celebrate it, for we have a wonderful gift. Some seeds which when planted will bring forth a very unusual

JOHNNY APPLESEED

apple tree. May we have a lunch for this journey?'

"Mother's eyes twinkled as she hastily placed in a small basket sandwiches and gingerbread.

"Johnny thanked her and away they went. After what seemed quite a walk for the small sturdy legs they halted in a grassy nook beside the brook.

" 'Here,' said the old man, 'is a grand place for your apple tree to grow.' And together they bored a hole in the rich earth.

"Jack knelt down and from his chubby hands dropped the beautiful brown seeds. Then he kissed his tiny palm and waved it over the hole as he cried:

" 'Good night, little seeds. Send me a little tree by and by when you wake up. I'll be waiting for it and will take good care of it.'

THE STORY OF

"They covered the seeds with the dark rich loam, then ate their lunch. Presently Jack was thirsty, and the old man fashioned a cup from a broad leaf and filled it at a near-by spring. Jack drank, and the little seeds also drank.

"Then the old man built a picket fence about the spot so no harm could come to it. As this was finished the bell on the corn barn told them dinner was ready.

"'Mudder,' cried Jack, bursting in to the house, 'we planted the seeds and the tree will be my own. Isn't that fine?'

"'Fine, indeed! I never heard of a better birthday present. It will last for years and years, and think of the fruit it will bear!'

"As the child ate he dreamed of the tree as it would be some day; full of rosy apples, and he was very proud of that magic spot beside the brook.

"Each day he ran out to look at it, and one

JOHNNY APPLESEED

morning he found the ground above the seeds humped up just a little. Another day the earth was cracked open, and soon after that to his great joy, he found a dear little sprig peeping up at him as though crying, 'Here I am! How do you do?'

"He danced about shouting for joy, and each day after that, could fairly see the little sprig turn into a tree.

"Johnny told him how the seeds sent tiny roots down into the earth and pushed the stem up through the ground, and Jack could hardly leave the spot which had now grown so dear.

"When the little tree was thirsty, the rain gave it drink. The kind wind blew and blew, bringing fresh sweet air for it to breathe, and with every whiff it seemed to swell.

"The spring sunshine warmed it down to its roots, and in time there were twigs with

THE STORY OF

leaf buds, which presently uncurled and opened wide.

"'See!' said Johnny, 'as the wind blows them they look like baby hands throwing kisses!'

"'Yeth!' cried Jack, 'maybe they are the kitheth I planted.'

"'To be sure,' Johnny replied, and together they watched it grow day after day, week after week, month after month.

"Jack's next birthday found the little tree a picture to behold. The trunk was sturdy, and on it there were many branches appearing here and there.

"Jack was quite a boy by this time, and soon after his little dresses were replaced by tiny trousers. His baby talk was no more, and he was now old enough to help care for the little tree.

"He dug about its roots with his wee spade, and Johnny showed him how to enrich the

JOHNNY APPLESEED

soil, and told him many things about the care of trees.

"It was so splendid to know that as the tree spread its branches in the air, so it spread its roots under the ground, giving it such a firm support the wind would have to be very strong indeed to blow it over.

" 'How does it drink?' the boy asked one day.

" 'Oh, such a fine way. It is a story all by itself,' replied Johnny. 'At the end of each root there are wee spongy mouths. When the rain comes they drink it and whisper "Run fast to the trunk."

" 'As it rushes through the trunk, the trunk cries in a gruff voice, "Run along to the branches."

" 'The branches wave and in sweet tones cry, "Welcome, run along to the twigs, they need you." The twigs drink it and whisper, "Run along to the stems; they are just waiting for you." The stems send it out to the tip end of the leaves as they wildly wave and laugh aloud over their sweet gift, for this water in the tree is sweet food that nourishes every part and is called sap.'

"This was a fine story, and every time it rained Jack watched the little tree, and thought he could almost hear the voices sending the moisture on and on.

"As time passed the tree became stronger and larger, and finally one spring day when Jack was quite a big boy he found buds on the branches.

" 'Buds!' he called in great excitement, and real buds they were, which the whole family came out to admire.

"The buds blossomed, and as the petals snowed down the air was sweet with their fragrance.

"When Jack found baby apples on his tree he wanted to celebrate, and Mother told him

"They looked like a lot of gnomes dressed for a party"

JOHNNY APPLESEED

that when they were ripe he could invite his friends and have an apple party.

"An apple party! That would be something new, and he hastened to tell the good news at school.

" 'They are wonderful apples,' he said. 'No one in this part of the country has any like them. I tell you we'll have the fun at that party. They are turning crimson; you never saw such a pretty apple tree!'

"A pretty tree it was indeed, and looked just like a Christmas tree all dressed up.

"One day Johnny pronounced the fruit ripe and ready to eat.

" 'Hurrah! To-morrow we can have the party,' cried Jack, tossing his cap into the air.

"Now the fun began. Mother baked all sorts of goodies, and the little home was made spick-and-span; even the door yard was swept for this occasion.

"The day dawned sweet and clear. After

THE STORY OF

breakfast Jack ran out to take one look at his beloved tree, but alas! What do you s'pose?

" 'What!' cried the audience in one breath.

"A cow had broken into the orchard, tramped the fence down, and was feasting on the rosy fruit! A few branches were broken, and a sorry sight it was, to be sure.

"Jack shrieked and threw himself on the ground sobbing:

" 'My dear little tree I planted with my own baby hands! I loved it so! Now it is ruined!'

"Johnny Appleseed heard the wail and hastened to the scene.

" 'It isn't ruined, Jack; it can be made almost as good as new. See!' He skilfully cut the broken branches, covered the wounded spots with a paste made of clay, talking the while to the little tree as though

JOHNNY APPLESEED

it were a person whose wounds he was binding up so carefully.

" 'See!' he said. 'This clay paste will harden and keep the bugs out of the wood until it can heal over. It will soon be all right again, but it is too bad. Such a picture as it was, and the apples are most all gone!'

"The apples!—Jack suddenly remembered. 'The apple party was to be to-day! What can we do?'

" 'Well, my boy, don't you worry. The apple party will be to-day just the same. We'll take this basket and I'll show you something I've kept as a surprise.

" 'I planted the seeds that were left over in the far corner lot, and those trees are as pretty a sight as you want to see. I have been watching them as we have this. Come along.'

"The two trudged on, Jack wiping away

his tears and beginning to wear a rainbow smile after the shower.

" 'It's a joke, isn't it?' he said. 'That cow had an apple party all by herself. I s'pose she didn't like it because I didn't invite her.

" 'Oh!' he exclaimed suddenly, 'there they are. How beautiful!'

"And indeed they were beautiful. A number of trees exactly like his own, all looking so thrifty, and the branches dotted with rosy fruit.

" 'We'll pick the apples and tie the stems to the branches of your own little tree, because that is where you planned to have your party,' said Johnny.

"Together they picked the apples, and with green string tied the stems to the branches of the little tree.

" 'You'd hardly know it happened!' cried the boy in joyous tones as the work was fin-

JOHNNY APPLESEED

ished, and both stood back to admire; and true it was, for the apples really seemed to be growing, and so the apple party was a success after all.

"The children had their lunch under the little tree, then each picked his own apple and ate it before you could say, 'Jack Robinson.'

" 'I know a great thing to do,' cried Jack, as they were about to throw away the core; 'save the seeds and plant them, and we'll all be Johnny Appleseeds. You'll each have a grand orchard started on your farm.'

" 'Splendid!' laughed the old man. 'If every seed brings forth a tree there will be great rejoicing when you take the apples to market, for they are certainly the best apples I ever tasted and should bring a good price.'

"Wild with excitement, the children trooped home, and before long the glossy

THE TALE OF THE

seeds were covered up in the ground, waiting for the wonderful thing that was to happen to them.

"In time there were many trees bearing the rosy fruit. All through one little boy having such a fine birthday party.

"A tree is the dearest of treasures. I mean any kind of tree. It does so many things. It gives fruit and shade. It gives the birds a place to build their homes, and in return you have their beautiful music all through the summer. It gives the squirrels a place to hide their nuts. From the trunk many insects find their food.

"If it were not for the trees there would be no mince pies. From the trees are built the ships which bring from foreign countries these many goodies. How could we have any houses, or any furniture to put in them, if there were no trees? See that splendid back log. It has kept us warm all the long

STOLEN DOLL CLOTHES

night. It came from a grand old tree that furnished fuel for many a winter fire.

"And now I must stop, for I fear my tale has been too long. If it has, please excuse me."

"How splendid!" chorused the audience. And little Allspice begged for another.

Nutmeg cried: "I know a grand one! It happened right in a forest near where I grew.

"You know those woods are full of monkeys, and they have great times. One of their traits is to mimic. They usually do what they see others do, and a good thing it was for the boy I'm going to tell you about.

"The boy's name was Enrico. He lived with his widowed mother at the edge of the forest. They were very poor and had tried in many ways to earn money without success.

"The mother was handy with her needle, and one day a neighbour child came in with her naked doll.

THE TALE OF THE

" 'I'll dress it,' said the mother, and from her scrap bag produced cloth which she soon fashioned into a quaint gown for the doll.

" 'Mother!' cried Enrico, much excited, 'there are many dolls in the town, without clothes. Could you not make them and I will sell them? I know I can.'

" 'We'll try,' said Mother. She emptied her purse, ran to the store, and soon returned heavily laden with gay materials, from which she fashioned coats, gowns, petticoats, bonnets, hats and all sorts of things for dolls.

"Enrico could scarcely wait for the time to come when he could go and try his luck at selling them. One morning he started with his basket well filled.

"His eyes shone, and his heart beat fast as he hurried along. He had to pass through the forest to reach the town. It was a long walk, and a hot day.

STOLEN DOLL CLOTHES

"'I think it is time to eat my lunch,' he presently said to himself as he sat down under the trees. He was obliged to empty the basket as the lunch was underneath the garments.

"He laid them in a neat pile and found the sandwiches and fruit which his mother had carefully prepared. He had barely finished when his head toppled over against a tree and he was fast asleep.

"And now comes the best part of the story. What do you think happened to those lovely doll clothes?"

"Don't stop!" cried Allspice. "Do tell us!"

"As the lad slept, there came a chattering and whisking about. In a moment dozens of monkeys came down from the trees. They gobbled up the crumbs, and then turned to the doll clothes. Almost before you could say 'Jack Robinson,' they were robed in the

THE TALE OF THE

tiny garments, and such a sight you never saw. They looked like a lot of gnomes dressed for a party. They played all sorts of games and raced wildly about in the greatest glee. Suddenly Enrico opened his eyes on the scene.

" 'The doll clothes. The doll clothes,' he wailed. 'Give them back!'

"The monkeys saucily nodded their heads and quickly climbed into the trees. Swinging from the branches with their tails curled about the limbs, they chattered as though crying, 'Get them if you can! Get them if you can!'

"This was serious, and Enrico sat watching and wondering what he could do, for he must have the clothes at once.

"Suddenly he remembered the monkey's desire to imitate. In the long ago his father had told him how they did just what they saw people do.

STOLEN DOLL CLOTHES

"It was worth trying, and the boy arose and threw off his cap.

"At once hats and bonnets were snowed down upon him. Enrico gathered them up and placed them in his basket.

"Then off came his coat. Coats of all sorts now dropped about him.

"Chuckling to himself, Enrico now removed his other garments, and immediately tumbled down the gay-coloured gowns and snowy underwear.

"Enrico gathered them up as fast as he could, fearing the monkeys might descend upon him and once more rob him of his treasures.

"He then dressed himself and hurried on. He found a ready sale for his wares in the market, and with a purse full of money, and requests for many more garments of the same sort, he hastened home to tell his mother of his good fortune.

TALE OF THE

"There was great rejoicing in the little home, and the day came when Enrico was selling doll clothes in his own little shop in the heart of the city.

"A dear little shop it was with a home in the back where his mother cooked and sewed on the dainty garments.

"Enrico never tired of telling the children who came to buy, how he almost lost the first lot of doll clothes he ever started out to sell."

General applause followed this interesting story, while the chairman cried, "Splendid! Splendid! It was most entertaining, and now I think the hour has arrived when we should hear from Beef and her creamy companion, both of whom remind me of Mary and her lamb, because where one goes the other follows."

The odd Brownie now came forward, with the creamy toddler holding fast to her hand. They both bowed, and the Brownie began:

"She loved her home"

BROWNIE DOLL

"I am commonly known as Beef, and I come not from the sheep or hog, but from the cow.

"As to where I come from, it would be hard to tell where I am not to be found, for I believe cows roam about over the whole world.

"You may ride on trains anywhere and everywhere; you may sail on boats; you may go up in flying machines, you will always see cows.

"I do not know of anything that seems quite as necessary as the cow, both for meat and for milk.

"I came from a certain cow that spent most of its time in a green meadow where birds sang above her head, and a near-by brook gurgled over the stones, making the sweetest music.

"Night and morning a maid came with a shiny pail on her arm; as she milked the

TALE OF THE

Bossy she sang to the accompaniment of the brook.

"Often two little children came, each with a silver cup, for a drink of the warm foaming milk.

"That cow was proud indeed to know that she furnished food for the little ones.

"She loved her home. She could hear the chickens clucking, the geese cackling, the lambs baaing, and the ponies neighing.

"She stood for hours looking off at the peaceful scene before her and seemed always content.

"Suddenly she found herself no more in the meadow but hanging in juicy quarters from a hook in a butcher shop. These quarters were cut up into various parts to be used for steaks, roasts, soup bones, beef tea, and all sorts of good things.

"At this time the store was trimmed up with bunches of green leaves and bright red

BROWNIE DOLL

berries. Scarlet Christmas bells nodded on all sides.

"It seemed to be a gay and festive scene. Sleigh bells jingled, telephones rang constantly, and finally I was placed in a basket with other goodies, and the next thing I knew I was flying over the snow in a bob sled.

"My basket was presently left on a kitchen table. Thereupon I was taken from the package. A fat lady gave me a poke with her finger, and nodded her head as she said:

"'Fine cut. Just right for my mince meat.' What that was I did not know, but I was placed in a kettle and bubbled around in hot water for some time, then I found myself in something else that was fastened to a table. A handle twirled and twirled, and I turned into a fine bunch of stuff, waiting for I knew not what.

"I'll have to tell you about my little

brother Suet, because he never could, he is so shy.

"I always noticed that when people bought beef, they chose the parts that had creamy fat clinging to them. They said they were sweeter and more tender, and that fat is this little brother of mine, and that's why he clings so closely to me. That's where he belongs.

"In a moment as I lay in the dish, all ground up, I felt coming down all over me wee bits of creamy fat, so you see he still followed me.

"I was much interested to know what mince meat was, and I kept my eyes and ears open to see what would happen next.

"It was a busy scene I looked out upon. One person was stoning raisins. Another was peeling apples. All sorts of spices were being ground. Citron was being cut up very fine, also orange and lemon peel. The vine-

BROWNIE DOLL

gar, molasses, and cider jugs were brought forth.

"Then everything was put into a wooden bowl, and as they were chopped they all seemed to be singing the merriest of tunes. By and by the mixture was tumbled into a crock with me, and I found I was beginning to swell and to be quite important. I was stirred and stirred, and then various people came and tasted and smacked their lips and tasted again. One said, 'A little more sugar, don't you think so?' Another looking very wise said, 'Needs more spice,' and so I was doctored and fussed with till finally I was pronounced just right, and I knew *the* time had arrived.

"I felt as one does at a circus when they have the grand entrée and I fairly held my breath as I waited for the next act. I was mince meat at last.

"Suddenly I was poured into what seemed

to be a round white blanket. It was so soft and cushiony I rejoiced over such a fate, but alas, another blanket was placed over me. There were no sheets on this bed, and it was as dark as a pocket. In a moment tiny eyelet holes appeared, from which I could peep through up into the eyes of the busy cook. Then a black door swung open. I was placed within a dark cavern, the door swung back, and all was still.

"I felt myself growing warmer and warmer. My bed turned from soft blankets to crispy covers. I bubbled and boiled, and presently when the cover was a golden brown the door flew open, and once more I came out into the light of day.

"I was placed in a window to cool, and the whole family came out to admire me. I felt so proud I could hardly keep still.

"I knew I was intended for some wonderful event. Mr. Cinnamon Stick, you said

BROWNIE DOLL

this pie was for the Christmas dinner to-morrow. Is it for an ornament or a decoration of some sort?"

"Ha! Ha! Ha! Ha!" sang the chorus, "you will soon learn when to-morrow comes what you will decorate."

"Why?" asked the Brownie, in alarm. "What will happen? What will they do with this pie?"

"Oh!" laughed Cinnamon Stick, "it's hard to tell; they *might* do any one of a number of things.

"It *might* be suspended on chains from the chandelier, and swing to the tune of an orchestra.

"They *might* start it rolling across the hardwood floor down that large hall, and wager whether it would fall upside down or downside up.

"There are many things that *might* be done with it, but what's the use of worrying about to-morrow. We still have much of the night to pass away.

"Here! what's this rolling across the floor?"

They all looked to see the pie itself rolling along mysteriously and silently. When it reached the hearth it spun round and round for a moment, then paused and began to speak.

"If you please, Mr. Chairman, and Ladies and Gentlemen, you are forgetting me, the most important part of the pie.

"I am the crust, and whoever heard of a pie of any kind without a crust? No one, of course, and so since I am really the most important member of the large family, I think I should have my turn."

"You certainly should!" cried Cinnamon Stick. "I am sorry I neglected to call you. We are glad, indeed, to hear your story. What are you made of?"

PIE CRUST

"I am composed of flour, lard, and water—"

"You'd be ruined if you didn't put a pinch of me in," cried Little Salt eagerly.

"Certainly I would. Thank you for not allowing me to be spoiled.

"Of course you all know flour is made from wheat. The wheat plant is a grass which looks much like barley and rye.

"The varieties are called, bearded, and beardless or bald.

"Some are planted in spring, for spring or summer wheat. Other kinds in the fall to be ready the next season, that is winter wheat. The latter was at one time thought to be the best, but lately with improved methods of manufacture the spring wheat is equally as good.

"There are two kinds, white and red. Of the winter wheat the white is best.

"Wheat is chiefly used for flour. The finest, but not the most wholesome, is nearest pure starch. The richer parts are found nearest the skin and are secured in the graham flour.

"Wheat has been known always, is mentioned in the Bible, and is found almost everywhere.

"China wheat is a spring wheat, and this is where it came from. Once upon a time some one had a chest of tea sent to him. It was a wonderful gift to have, and was highly prized. In that tea was found a curious grain. No one knew what it was, but they decided to plant it. From that came wheat, and was called spring wheat.

"If you have been in the country you know how the wheat is cut with big machines, and taken to the barn.

"Then many men appear and they thresh it. That means to get the chaff, the outer

PIE CRUST

husk, off. Then the grain is taken to the mill and ground into flour.

"The flour is used for bread, cake, pies, and almost all of the baked stuff we have.

"Lard is made from pork fat. The fat is boiled or rendered.

"Water is composed of two parts of hydrogen and one of oxygen, commonly called H_2O. Pure water can be obtained by distillation from the ocean, as is often done at sea. Some towns on the South American Coast have been supplied in this way.

"The chief source of supply for water which falls on the earth is from the ocean. The heat of the sun raises a vapour from its surface. This vapour condenses and falls as rain or snow, either on sea or land. Rain after falling for some time is almost pure and for that reason is called soft. Hard water contains various minerals.

HOW JACK FILLED

"That's all about the crust. It isn't very interesting, nor funny, but it is good and everybody loves it."

"Indeed, it is good, and most necessary to every pie," declared the Cinnamon Doll.

"And now suppose we wish for the Story Sprite. She is a dear and we have time for just one more story."

This wish was hardly expressed when the sound of bells was heard and there before them stood the Story Lady, bringing with her a joyous shower of bells.

"Oh, my dearies, this is the last time I can come!

"It is Christmas, as you know, and many Christmas parties are awaiting me, but I just had to keep my promise to you.

"This time I want to tell you a Christmas tale I am sure you will enjoy and love.

It is called:

THE STOCKINGS

HOW JACK FILLED THE STOCKINGS.

"It was Christmas Eve. The younger children were snugly tucked in bed, while Jack sat staring at the empty stockings swinging from the mantel shelf in the gleaming firelight.

"Jack was only twelve, and the man of the house. His face was very grave as he gazed alternately at the stockings, then at his mother bustling about tidying up the room.

"She finally sat down, declaring sadly: 'It's no use, Jack. I haven't a penny to spare; the stockings will have to go empty.'

"The boy spoke not a word, but watched the fire sputter and crackle as though perhaps it might solve the problem.

"Of one thing he was certain: the stockings should not go empty if he could help it.

"The fire *did* show him the way, for sud-

HOW JACK FILLED

denly the logs began to send out tiny sparks and snap for all the world like popcorn.

"'Mother!' he cried suddenly, 'I have an idea. I'm going out.'

"'Dress warm then, dear, and good luck to you.'

"The boy hurried out into the night, and *such* a night!

"Snowflakes were flying thick and fast, and above his head the ice-coated trees spread their friendly branches. He loved the crisp, sharp air, and raised his face that the flakes might lodge and sting.

"Soon he reached the busy street and watched keenly for a chance to earn a dime.

"Suddenly he saw a woman carrying a suitcase, running for the car, while at her side toddled a child trying in vain to keep up with her.

"'Let me help, may I?' asked Jack wistfully.

"He chose the busiest corner where there was a wonderful

THE STOCKINGS

"'Oh, if you only would,' replied the woman, grateful indeed for the aid.

"As they reached the corner she slipped a silver piece into his hand. The car stopped, then whizzed on, leaving Jack staring at the quarter, hardly able to believe it.

"'A good beginning,' he murmured, and ran into a near-by store, where he purchased a few ears of popcorn and a small jar of molasses.

"Mother, much surprised, welcomed the gifts and boy with open arms.

"'I earned them, Mother! Make some corn balls and candy while I try again,' and away he went.

"This time he was not so successful. Every one seemed busy and hurried past him, not even glancing at the eager, earnest face.

"On one corner a hand-organ man was grinding out his music. Jack watched to see

HOW JACK FILLED

the people stop and drop pennies into his little cup.

"Suddenly the boy had an inspiration. He could sing like a bird. In fact he had been soloist of a boy choir in the town where they had lived before coming to the city.

"That work he loved, and was never so happy as, when clothed in his robes, walking up the aisle, singing while the great splendid organ pealed out its glorious music.

"One song, the Christmas Lullaby, was his special favourite. He always sang it at Christmas time. Why not sing it here on the street?

"It was sweeter than hand-organ music, and surely people ought to be willing to give a few pennies to hear it.

"No sooner thought than done, and Jack darted down the street a few blocks away from the hand-organ man.

"He chose the busiest corner where there

THE STOCKINGS

was a wonderful toy store. In the window was a tree covered with gifts. The lights twinkled and danced as though cheering him on, and so there he paused and sang.

"He was a beautiful child. Indeed, in the fashionable church at home he had been called the Christ child, and now as he sang, many were attracted by his face and the clear sweet tones.

"They listened and passed on, leaving in the shabby cap many bits of silver.

"After a time the boy walked on, halting at various corners to sing, and presently found himself in front of a church.

"The music of the great organ pierced the air and as the door swung to and fro, he saw a large audience with many children gaily dressed, waiting expectantly.

"Jack was tired and cold. He longed to be enfolded in the light and warmth within and listen to the music, and he quietly crept inside up a stairway, then down to the front. No one was there and he leaned forward to see a wonderful tree. It sparkled with tinsel, while coloured lights gleamed here and there like shining jewels breathing a halo about the head of the Christmas Angel standing on the topmost branch.

"The outstretched arms seemed to pronounce a blessing on the fruit of this tree waiting to be showered on the many little ones, who stood admiring and exclaiming over this vision of beauty.

"It was an enormous tree. The top branches were fastened securely to a heavy pole which was thrown across the chancel and rested in the grooves on the hand-carved posts which stood either side of the entrance to this sacred place.

"Jack, fascinated by the scene, watched hungrily every detail, and as a thirsty flower holds up its dainty head for the first rain-

THE STOCKINGS

drops, so the boy eagerly drank in every note of the music which he knew so well.

"He longed to be a choir boy once more, but he was timid and bashful and feared to make any effort in this direction in a strange city.

"As he pondered on how to gain the coveted position, he watched the tree being stripped of its fruit and placed in many outstretched hands.

"He gazed wistfully on the joyous scene, but was suddenly startled by a flash of light, which, from his position, he saw was a thread of flame leaping upwards toward the Christmas Angel.

"There was but one thing to do, and he was the one to do it. Without a thought for himself he sprang for the pole, hung by his toes, and in an instant the flaming branch was broken from the tree and crushed in his hands.

HOW JACK FILLED

"Below a quick cry of 'Fire!' rang out, then was heard the shriek of a child.

"Jack knew the impending panic must be averted instantly, and as he swung up on to the pole, he wound his limbs about it, and there perched in the topmost branches, a veritable Christ Child, he sang, as he never sang before, the Christmas Lullaby.

"The cries below ceased. The audience stared in amazement. Had he fallen from the blue skies painted on the ceiling by a master hand or had one of the Murillo angels, hovering amongst the billowy clouds, come to life?

"Those who heard never forgot the pathos of the plaintive melody.

"The choirmaster listened breathlessly, for here was the soloist he had for months been vainly seeking.

"The organist, wild with delight over the

THE STOCKINGS

heavenly music, coming from he knew not where, followed gently with the organ accompaniment, the flute-like tones blending with the bird notes of the boy.

"Higher and higher soared the voice of the Christmas Angel, while the people gazed entranced. Such tender sweetness it had never been their privilege to hear.

"Surely the Baby Jesus was being lulled to sleep by the angelic music, which at last slowly and gently died away.

"A moment of tense silence was followed by a rustle; the tension was broken and Jack swung himself back to the gallery, to be greeted by many outstretched hands.

"He had many questions to answer and before the child realised it, he had told the story of limp stockings hanging by the chimneyside at home, and how hard he had tried to fill them.

TALE OF THE

"His pathetic tale, together with his daring efforts to quench the fire and avert a panic, moved many to tears.

"You all know what followed. How he was driven home in state in a grand sleigh drawn by a pair of prancing horses, and how his new-found friends not only filled the stockings, but then and there engaged him as soloist of the boy choir at such a salary that his mother need work no more, and they were all comfortable and happy for many a day.

"And now good-bye, and I wish you a very Merry Christmas."

With that the Story Elf vanished, and her audience chorused:

"Wasn't that lovely?"

"Indeed, it was," declared Mr. Cinnamon Stick; "and now I believe we have heard from every one of this large family—"

"No, you haven't! No, you haven't!" cried a sprightly voice, and there appeared

INTERROGATION POINT

the queerest figure imaginable, coming apparently up from the floor like a Jack in the box.

He seemed to be a combination of every one of them, and before he had even spoken he seemed to be asking a question.

"Look at me. Guess who I am."

"An Interrogation Point," announced the Vinegar Doll.

"Yes, but an Interrogation Point asks a question. Who can answer it?"

The dolls leaned forward curiously examining this figure.

His head seemed made of suet, and he wore a hat adorned with tiny beef croquettes about the edge of the brim. Sprays of raisins and currants wandered over the crown, and about his neck was a necklace of allspice with dangles of cloves, cinnamon and nutmegs.

Pepper and salt sprinkled his clothing,

TALE OF THE

which seemed made from orange and lemon peel. About his waist was a queer girdle from which wee sugar bowls, molasses jugs and vinegar cruets jingled together, while he tossed gay coloured apples into the air, caught them skilfully and then disposed of them in various pockets.

With a gay nod he cried, "Can no one answer the question? Let me tell you a little about myself, and then perhaps you can.

"You have all told how necessary you are. Let me tell you there would never have been a mince pie without me, nor anything else worth while.

"Let me ask of you growing things, how did you happen to grow? How did any of you happen to be? Some one had to plant the seeds. Some one had to take care of the trees, vines and shrubs after they started to grow.

INTERROGATION POINT

"Where there was no rain, water had to be carried. The trees and vines had to be tended, trimmed, and cultivated. When the fruit was finally ready, it had to be packed and shipped all over the world.

"Even after it found its way into that kitchen, what happened? Everybody was—what—what was everybody doing? Now do tell me what this interrogation point stands for? Think!" he pleaded.

Everybody thought. They screwed up their faces and thought some more. They took one foot out from under them and thought. They put the other foot under them and thought again.

What was everybody doing to get the pie ready—chopping, grinding, baking.

Suddenly everybody beamed and chorused: "Working! Everybody was working! You are called Work!"

"To be sure I am, and a lot of work it took

to make this pie. All over the world many, many people had many busy days.

"Can't you just see them picking the raisins; sugaring the citron; grinding spice; cutting the wheat; packing the oranges; taking care of the cow; gathering the apples, and crushing them in the mill for cider?

"Oh, my dears, there is always work. Johnny Appleseed did an endless amount of work, and see what came from it.

"The one who packed that box of tea and happened to drop a grain of wheat therein, did a wonderful thing. That tiny grain brought us a kind of wheat we might never have had. Can't you just see them planting that tiny seed? They watched it grow, tending the little sprout till it finally came to maturity, and more grains were planted. At last there was a wonderful crop of wheat, all due to your humble servant Work."

With a sunny nod he vanished, and they

"Best pie you ever made, my dear"

INTERROGATION POINT

looked and listened, but not even a clank of his girdle charms did they hear.

"Well! Well!" cried Cinnamon. "Wasn't he fine? Who would ever have thought of him as belonging to mince pie. I fear we were all forgetting that most important point, and glad I am he remembered to appear. And now, my dears, the dawn is breaking, we must return."

"But the mouse!" cried timid Allspice. "What about the mouse?"

"Oh, yes, the mouse!" chorused the audience breathlessly. "What about the mouse?"

Cinnamon Stick said no word, but pointed a long thin finger toward the clock.

The clock struck one (which was really half-past five), the mouse ran down, and the chain clinkety clanked as he hopped to the floor and ran away to his hole, and was seen no more.

His disappearance seemed a signal, and at once was heard a joyful chorus. As the dolls sang they formed a procession, and two by two marched back to the clock and wound their way about the spiral columns.

The Pie Crust was at the head and settled down in the pan, its cover upheld as by an invisible hand. The dolls jumped into their places, the cover was slowly dropping, when suddenly up popped the head of the Vinegar Cruet.

"The Gifts!" he cried. "You forgot the Gifts!"

At that up popped every other head, crying in chorus:

"The Gifts! The Gifts! You forgot the Gifts!"

"No, I didn't forget. They are on the way."

As Mother and Jack watched, suddenly a red-coated, white, fur-trimmed figure ap-

INTERROGATION POINT

peared. On his back was a basket piled high with candy. He made his way to the clock, and as he stood over the pie he cried in the jolliest of tones:

"Open your mouths and shut your eyes, and I'll give you something to make you wise."

Open popped the dolls' mouths, looking like a lot of birds, each waiting for a worm, and all were filled to the brim with sweets.

They then nestled down close together. The top crust settled in place. The flames flickered and died out; then all was still.

The next day was crisp and bright. Father came, and a joyous time they all had over their gifts.

The turkey dinner was delicious, and presently the mince pie appeared in all its glory.

Such a beautiful mince pie as it was!

Jack watched Mother cut it, and listened

BEST PIE EVER MADE

breathlessly for the "Ha! Ha! Ha's," and the "Ho! Ho! Ho's," but not a sound did he hear, till presently at the first mouthful Father cried:

"Best pie you ever made, my dear. For once you have it sweet enough!"

Jack and his mother merely nodded and smiled, but not a word said they!

THE END

Milton Keynes UK
Ingram Content Group UK Ltd.
UKHW020638261023
431376UK00007B/327